Only the extraordinary women of Athena Academy could create Oracle—a covert intelligence organization so secret that not even its members know who else belongs. Now it's up to three top agents to bring down the enemies who threaten all they've sworn to protect....

Kim Valenti:
An NSA cryptologist, this analytical genius and expert code breaker is the key to stopping a deadly bomb.
COUNTDOWN by Ruth Wind—April 2005

Diana Lockworth:
With only twenty-four hours until the president's inauguration, can this army intelligence captain thwart an attempt to assassinate him?
TARGET by Cindy Dees—May 2005

Selena Jones:
Used to ensuring international peace, this legal attaché has her biggest assignment yet—foiling a terrorist attack abroad.
CHECKMATE by Doranna Durgin—June 2005

Dear Reader,

What's hot this spring? Silhouette Bombshell! We're putting action, danger, romance and that exhilarating feeling of winning against the odds right at your fingertips.

Feeling wild? *USA TODAY* bestselling author Lindsay McKenna's *Wild Woman* takes you to Hong Kong for the latest story in the SISTERS OF THE ARK miniseries. Pilot Jessica "Wild Woman" Merrill is on a mission to infiltrate the lair of a criminal mastermind—but she's been thrown a curveball in the form of an unexpected partner....

The clock is ticking as an NSA code breaker races to stop a bomb in *Countdown* by Ruth Wind, the latest in the high-octane ATHENA FORCE continuity series. This determined Athena woman will risk her career and even kidnap an FBI bomb squad member to save the day!

Indiana Jones and Lara Croft have nothing on modern legend Veronica Bright, the star of author Sharron McClellan's *The Midas Trap*. Veronica has a chance to find the mythical Midas Stone—but to succeed, she's got to risk working for a man who tried to ruin her years ago....

Meet CPA Whitney "Pink" Pearl, heroine of *Show Her the Money* by Stephanie Feagan. Blowing the whistle on a corporate funny-money scam lands her in the red, but Pink won't let death threats, abduction attempts or steamy kisses from untrustworthy lawyers get in the way of justice!

Please send your comments to me c/o Silhouette Books, 233 Broadway, Suite 1001, New York, NY 10279.

Sincerely,

Natashya Wilson
Associate Senior Editor, Silhouette Bombshell

Please address questions and book requests to:
Silhouette Reader Service
U.S.: 3010 Walden Ave., P.O. Box 1325, Buffalo, NY 14269
Canadian: P.O. Box 609, Fort Erie, Ont. L2A 5X3

COUNTDOWN
RUTH WIND

BOMBSHELL™

Published by Silhouette Books

America's Publisher of Contemporary Romance

Special thanks and acknowledgment
are given to Ruth Wind for her contribution
to the ATHENA FORCE series.

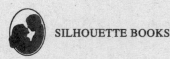 **SILHOUETTE BOOKS**

ISBN 0-373-51352-6

COUNTDOWN

www.SilhouetteBombshell.com

Printed in U.S.A.

RUTH WIND

is the award-winning author of both contemporary and historical romance novels. She lives in the mountains of the Southwest with her two growing sons and many animals in a hundred-year-old house that the town blacksmith built. The only hobby she's had since she started writing is tending the ancient garden of irises, lilies and lavender beyond her office window, and she says she can think of no more satisfying way to spend a life than growing children, books and flowers. Ruth Wind also writes women's fiction under the name Barbara Samuel. You can visit her Web site at www.barbarasamuel.com.

For my son Ian,
who helped a lot with this book.
Thanks, kiddo!

Prologue

It was night and snowing when Kim Valenti parked at FBI headquarters in Chicago. Snow came in through the window of the stolen car—a 1971 gold Buick Skylark—that she'd hot-wired at the parking lot of the UBC television station. She'd be glad to get somewhere warmer.

Before she got out, she checked her face in the rearview mirror. If there was blood showing, she would draw attention to herself, and someone would be concerned or alarmed, which would cause more delays. She couldn't risk losing any more time.

There was a bomb ticking away at the airport. Somewhere. Due to detonate in exactly—she checked her watch—seventy-nine minutes.

In the mirror, she saw that her lip was swollen. She'd have a black eye tomorrow. A few scrapes, but no damage that would make her stand out too much in a law enforcement agency.

She got out of the car and hid the gun she'd also stolen in the small of her back, tucked into the waistband of her jeans. The weight of it was comforting and cold. Her cell phone was in her hand, the cord around her wrist.

Snow fell more heavily now, and she was halffrozen from the drive through the Chicago streets in a broken-down car with a shattered window.

In spite of the cold, her torn and battered ear throbbed. She wished it *would* have frozen. At least that would make it stop hurting. Without breaking stride, she scooped a handful of snow from the hood of a nearby car and pressed the icy ball to torn cartilage.

As she approached the front doors of the FBI building, a group of men erupted into the parking lot, rushing toward cars and vans. They shouted directions to one another, pulled on gloves, carted cases and rifles.

All headed, no doubt, for the television station. Kim ducked into the shadow of a truck, watching, her mouth hard. She could tell them that their rush was futile, but they wouldn't listen to her now any more than they had earlier.

No, if she had any chance of success, there was only one man for the job—Lex Tanner, FBI explosives expert and a compatriot she'd believed in before this morning.

She spied him toward the back of the group, carrying a metal suitcase. His dark hair was cut very short, the nose surprisingly recognizable from the pictures she'd seen, and he was quite tall. At least six-four. Rangy, lean and muscled, with shoulders big enough to shelter her from the wind.

As he neared her spot, she stepped out of the shadows. "Lex Luthor, I presume?"

He started, narrowing his eyes and sizing her up. Recognition washed over his features. "Valenti?" He looked more alarmed than pleased. "Where the hell have you been? I've been calling all afternoon."

"Long story. Right now, I need you to bring your little bomb kit and come with me to the airport."

"I can't. I'm on my way to UBC. There's a terrorist—"

"Yeah, yeah—" she waved a hand "—never mind. That's not the problem."

"They've stolen a bomb they're threatening to detonate—"

"It's not at the station."

"They've got hostages."

"I know." She took a breath. "Look, I don't have

time to explain everything, but the drama at UBC is a smoke screen—the bomb is at the airport."

"It's not there! Don't you get it? We've been over it a hundred and forty-seven times." His exasperation might have been understandable if they'd been strangers.

If he hadn't seen that she was extremely skilled. If he didn't know better.

If she hadn't proved herself by trusting his instincts, sight unseen.

If, if, if. She shook her head. She could stand here and argue, wasting time, explaining, or she could—

She pulled out her gun, using her body to shield it from the sight of the others, and poked the barrel into his ribs. "I didn't want to do it this way, but you won't listen."

"What—?"

She glared at him. "Don't make me hurt you, Luthor. I liked you until today."

"This is crazy." He glanced toward the men entering their trucks.

"Don't even think about it." She jabbed the butt into his ribs, harder. "I am dead serious."

"You're going to fuck up your career doing this."

Kim met his eyes. They were extremely blue. She'd read somewhere that extremely blue or green eyes showed a highly sexual nature.

Furious was more the word at the moment.

Oh, well. "Get in the car and I'll explain."

"You won't shoot me. I know you won't."

"I won't *kill* you," she said. "But I will hurt you if you don't come with me. Now." She pushed harder.

He resisted. "Explain."

She met his eyes with an icy lift of her own eyebrow. "Walk."

He glanced over his shoulder. No one was looking at them. Kim nudged him. "I tried to go through channels, but none of you has given me the respect I deserve, and because of that, people may die unnecessarily."

"If I go against orders, I'll be fired."

"I'm not talking anymore."

For an instant longer, he resisted. His nostrils flared in fury.

"It's killing you to have to listen to a girl, isn't it?"

"No, I—"

"My mother was a nurse in Vietnam. Did you know that? She was taken hostage once for three days, and it's something that has given her nightmares the rest of her life."

"Why the *hell* would I care, Valenti?"

"Because you can trust that I am very, *very* sincere when I say that I hate the whole hostage game. I would do *anything* to free hostages—but I won't let other people die. Do you understand?"

He narrowed his eyes, the jaw still mulish. Damn. She really did not want to hurt him. She would if she had to, but it would be messier and she needed him.

"Luthor, I've had a very bad night. My ear is killing me. There are a couple of bastards at that television station who may or may not kill hostages, but there are law enforcement officials on scene to deal with them. They also don't have a bomb at the station, and that's what I need you for."

"How is it, *Kim,* that you're so much smarter than the entire federal law enforcement community?"

She blinked. "I don't know, *Lex.* You tell me. Maybe I'm just smart. One thing I know for sure is that I *do* know what I'm talking about because—by the way did I tell you I speak Arabic fluently?—I overheard them talking at the television station. There is a bomb or a suicide bomber headed for the airport or *at* the airport, and people will die if we don't go now. I don't know how to defuse a bomb. You do."

"You finished?"

"Yes."

"Let's go. You can explain the rest in the car."

Chapter 1

Somehow, Kim Valenti fell asleep next to her lover. It was not something she ordinarily allowed. Maybe it was the long days trying to break a troublesome code. Maybe it was the cold, nearly winter night. Maybe just general weariness. Whatever.

She slept.

Hard.

And as often happened these days, the nightmares came. Jason, laughing and joking, his big hands and goofy smile—suddenly beheaded. A casualty of war.

He'd been a professional soldier, after all. Sometimes soldiers died in the line of duty.

The dream yanked her out of sleep, her hands raised, her legs thrashing, a yell of protest on her lips. This time, her lover caught her in his sturdy arms.

"Hey," Marc said quietly. "You okay?"

Blinking, shuddering as if she'd nearly fallen off a cliff, Kim wiped her face. "Yeah."

Kim's mother, Eileen, had been plagued by nightmares throughout Kim's childhood, and the children had learned never to awaken her in the usual way, by grabbing a shoulder or an elbow. If she fell asleep on the couch after work, they'd simply stand beside her and call her name quietly until she stirred. To do otherwise was to risk a sharp fist to the face as the soldier she'd been reacted to a threat long past.

Now that she'd lost a son to war, Eileen said she never dreamed at all anymore. Kim had wearily confessed one night, over plates of pasta, that she'd taken it on for her mother. She had regular nightmares about her brother Jason. Her mother had squeezed her shoulder. *Sorry, sweetheart.*

"Argh!" Kim said, rubbing her eyes. "It's this damned code! It's driving me nuts!"

"You're having nightmares about codes?"

She shook her head. "Not exactly." She couldn't discuss it. Her brother's death was something she didn't talk about, and the code was something she wasn't allowed to discuss with a civilian.

The two things were feeding into each other tonight: Jason, dead in Iraq two years ago, and the Arabic code running through her mind. Endless ribbons of delicate, graceful lettering flowing across the back of her eyelids. Over and over. Almost clicking into place, then sliding away from her.

Kim swore. She wasn't going to be getting any sleep tonight. Even less if she didn't get rid of her lover.

"We're not supposed to be doing this anyway," she said, easing away from him. "No sleeping over."

He groaned, and buried his well-chiseled face into the pillow. Glossy black hair splashed over the white linens. His shoulders, round and smooth, stuck out of the sheet. "Don't make me go."

"You know the rules."

Marc faced her. "What would it hurt if I slept over just once?"

"*Nyet*, nope, not a chance." She rolled away, slid into the robe she'd left at the foot of her bed. As she tied it, she tried to soften up her line a little bit. "You don't want this to get serious any more than I do. We'd make each other crazy in a week."

He rubbed his perfectly grizzled jaw. "I know, I know."

She liked Marc just fine. He was a safe, warm companion, who made her laugh. They'd dated off and on for more than two years, and neither of them saw anyone else, particularly, but they didn't intend to be serious. No one in his life knew she existed, and no one in hers knew he did. They kept company, sometimes made love, kept each other on track about getting too serious. They were both very ambitious and had no intentions of getting sidetracked from their careers into something as ordinary as love and marriage.

If he'd had a few more brains, he might have been good long-term material, but his IQ just about matched his job: he was a model for a major men's clothing line. Beautiful to be sure, but not someone she felt she could trust for the long haul. It was the perfect arrangement for the short haul.

Marc buried his face. Made a noise. Kim slapped his very nicely shaped butt. "Get moving."

"C'mon. Have a heart." He reached out a big hand with elegantly manicured nails that somehow managed to look rugged anyway. "I'm tired, Kim. Really. It's cold out there. This bed is so comfortable."

She headed for the bathroom. "Nope. You've got to get moving because I've got to work."

"Work? It's nearly midnight. Won't it wait until morning?"

"No. Do you want a shower?"

"No, thanks." Reluctantly, he tossed the covers off and stood up, stretching. Kim allowed herself to admire him. Too bad he wasn't brighter, she thought wryly. He was Italian, handsome, kind, and she had no doubt he'd be a good father. And she could look at him for hours. Trouble was most women could, and he'd age well. She suspected he would be married many times as the years went by.

Just a gut feeling.

He put on his jeans and wandered over to put his arms around Kim. He kissed her neck. "Thanks for a great evening. You know I'm crazy about you."

She patted his hands, allowed the kiss. "Yeah, yeah, Spinuzzi."

Against her neck, he asked quietly, "Did you have a good time, Kim?"

It was unexpectedly vulnerable. Kim cursed inwardly. One of these days, she was going to have to remember that men were not as tough as they wanted women to think they were.

She turned and kissed him. "Always, Marc. I enjoy your company, and you're a great guy. We're just not couple material and you know it."

He squeezed her shoulder and nodded. "You're right, you're right. Go take your shower and I'll call you in a few days."

"Thanks."

After a hot shower, Kim made a peanut butter sandwich and a cup of hot chocolate and carried them into her study.

"Alone at last," she breathed, tugging her thick hair into a knot at the nape of her neck. She settled her cup and slid her chair up to the computer. Code rolled relentlessly through the back of her brain. Insistent, incoherent. Strings of garbled letters, Arabic and English, back and forth. She squeezed her eyes shut and let go of a sigh.

As a code breaker for the National Security Agency, Kim was trying to decrypt a group of e-mails suspected to have originated with a terrorist network called Q'rajn. The NSA had intercepted dozens of missives over the past few weeks, and the flurry had turned into a blizzard of e-mails the past three days. Kim, along with her partner, Scott Shepherd, had been working for weeks nonstop to find the key. With the increased activity, there was increasing dread.

Something nagged her tonight, a sense of something glimpsed out of the corner of her eye, something visible only in peripheral vision. She wanted another look at the code, to see if that jarred anything loose.

Her study was a plain room with open desks and two computers. The blinds were drawn. It was quiet so late. Her neighbors were largely young professionals like herself, with jobs in the local "alphabet agencies"—CIA, NSA, FBI—or the military installations in and around Washington, D.C., and Baltimore.

While she waited for the computers to boot, Kim ate her sandwich and admired the view of her kitchen from the office chair. A large jade plant stood on the windowsill, and on the wall behind the table was an enormous red-and-black Navajo blanket. It had been a gift from her mentor and reminded her of the time she'd spent at the Athena Academy for the Advancement of Women in Arizona. Athena educated girls ages ten to eighteen, at a state-of-the-art facility where girls trained in academics, martial arts, languages and other leadership skills.

Kim was proud of her little condo. Few women in her traditional Italian family lived on their own, even when they were twenty-five, as Kim was. Even fewer lived outside the enclave in Baltimore known as Little Italy. Not one of them had purchased real estate, not on her own.

It was one of the first goals Kim had made and met. The modern, two-bedroom condo was not particularly notable, though she loved the big windows and the master bedroom loft, but it was all hers. All modern convenience and post-turn-of-the-century architecture, which she'd decorated in a bright, coral-and-turquoise Southwestern theme. Some locals thought it was kitschy—so "last year," as one friend had said—but for Kim, it was a reminder of the things she'd learned in the harsh and beautiful world of the desert. So much of who she was came from those days outside of Phoenix.

As she waited for her computer to load various programs and go through the virus checks, she switched on the radio that sat on the corner of her desk. The dial was tuned to a world music station that

played a variety of Latin, African and European se-
lections. The switches helped keep her awake.

Usually.

When the computers were up and running, she
clicked on the icons to download e-mail on both
machines.

Kim had three e-mail addresses—one for personal mail on her home computer, one for NSA-
related material, which had a dedicated line the government paid for.

A third address was used strictly to receive e-mail
from a top-secret, outside agency, called Oracle. It
was located on her personal machine, to avoid any
cross-contamination from work.

On the work computer, she dialed into the government network, where she would be able to explore the files connected to the current case. It was
sometimes laborious signing in, but tonight the computer whizzed through the screens, the layers and
layers of security designed to thwart hackers.

Most of them, anyway. No system was entirely
safe, no matter what the government wanted to believe. They did their best. It was a fairly tight system,
and whenever a weakness was discovered, computer
security experts were on the spot to fix it.

On her home computer, the personal e-mails
sorted into one folder. Twenty-seven, which was a
lot for her in one day. She frowned. She'd check
them in a minute, but first she switched IDs and

asked the computer to fetch her Oracle e-mails. Maybe they'd have something to help crack this code.

Oracle was a special computer system developed to track information gathered from FBI, CIA, NSA and military databases, to be then cross-checked and matched. Created in the days before Homeland Security, it had been developed to help avoid disasters like Pearl Harbor and the 1993 Trade Center bombing, events that might have been prevented had key information been shared between agencies.

Kim had been recruited through AA.gov, a Web site connecting Athena Academy grads and students. She assumed Oracle was run by someone within the school network, and she knew there were a handful of operatives in key organizations—such as Kim and her work with the NSA—but all were protected by a cloak of anonymity. No one knew the agents. No one outside of Oracle knew it existed. It worked beyond the map of security in the U.S. government.

After Homeland Security had been created, Oracle had theoretically become obsolete.

Theoretically.

In fact, Oracle had not disbanded because it provided a fail-safe for the other organizations. Although she didn't know the particulars, she knew Oracle agents were able to get a fix on problems and provide evidence to thwart troublesome activities before the agencies involved were able to act. It was not infallible any more than any other device, but it helped prevent information from slipping between the cracks.

The folder for Oracle mail was labeled simply Delphi. It only received e-mail sporadically, and always from the same place. Tonight, it showed one new message.

Tonight, Kim fervently hoped for some information about Q-group, and she clicked on the folder. The e-mail read:

To: Ariadne@orcl.org
From: Delphi@orcl.org
Subject: q's
1. Intelligence reports Q'rajn definitely tied to Berzhaan. CIA has tracked operatives overseas. FBI reports activity within the United States, links to Berzhaan terrorist community.
2. Two names emerging in connection with current activities: Fathi bin Amin Mansour and Hafiz abu Malik Abd-Humam, both natives of Berzhaan.
-Mansour is prodigiously intelligent. Advanced degrees from Oxford in chemical engineering and European history. Mother and two brothers killed in guerilla raids by the Kemini rebels four years ago, for which he holds the West responsible. He is connected to several bombings. His whereabouts are unknown. See attached photograph, taken in London, 2001.
-Abd-Humam is an associate of Mansour's father, a professor without overt terrorist ties. Appears to

be a devoted family man, religious but not overtly
so. He has protested Western (particularly U.S.) involvement in Berzhaan politics and has written
papers supporting self-determination for his
country. His connection is not yet known. There
are no known photos at this time.
Delphi

The attached photo showed a man in his early fifties, impeccably dressed in a dark business suit. His
face was dominated by large, dark eyes and an intense expression, and Kim imagined that he generally received more than a cursory second glance from
most women.

Kim copied the e-mail into a word-processing
program, removed all header information and printed
a copy. Then she destroyed the e-mail, both through
the delete key and a more sophisticated function designed to erase it entirely from the hard drive. If she
were investigated or hacked, there would be no trace
of Oracle on her computer.

Taking the paper from the printer, she sipped her
hot chocolate, thinking. Maybe the names themselves would offer a clue toward the code pattern.

Were there possibilities in the names? Abd-
Humam was a common surname, but it had religious
overtones: servant of the high-minded. Mansour was
a very common name. She scowled, trying to remember. She was fluent in Arabic, as well as Italian,

French, and—through a lovely triangle of events the year she was twelve—Navajo. But one didn't remember everything.

With a pad of paper and a pencil, she scribbled more notes, played with possibilities, fixed the English, then the Arabic letters in her mind. Something for the wheels to spin around as she slept.

She rubbed her eyes wearily. Q'rajn was a very dangerous organization, as they'd proven more than once with all the usual—though no less horrifying— earmarks of fanaticism: suicide bombings and death threats and displays of bravado in villages across the Middle East. They always faded away before they could be captured, though the CIA had been lucky in nabbing a key player last summer. He'd not given up much information, but his background and connections had provided some genuine leads and links to terrorism in Berzhaan.

"Okay, let's try something else," she said aloud, and keyed in her code to open the work files, and ran sample lines from several e-mails through a mechanical translator: Arabic to English, English to Arabic. Arabic and English combined, one sentence in one language, the next every other word, the next the first language, just to see what might turn up.

Computers at the NSA were busy running the encrypted material—dozens of intercepted e-mails— through programs of various sorts, checking logarithms and structures and known patterns. It was also checking another series of possibilities that Kim had programmed.

Nothing so far.

She slumped in the chair and picked up a bottle of eyedrops from the desk. Leaning back, she dropped Visine into her dry eyes. The shift in position eased the tight muscles in her neck and she stayed there a minute, her chin pointed at the ceiling. Her eyes were closed. The room was quiet.

The agency was sometimes too crazy for her. At home there were no ringing phones, no jokes between members of the team, no one having a low, fierce argument with a spouse over a cell phone connection.

Around her, Kim heard only the breathing of her computers and above that a respectful female voice reading the headlines on the radio. It was the fourth time she'd heard the news since dinner, so she didn't pay a lot of attention, but kept one ear open for anything new or notable. With such a blizzard of encoded e-mails, she was uneasy. Something was coming.

The newscaster said, "Fourteen people were killed when a train derailed near Munich this afternoon. A terrorist cell in the Sudan claimed responsibility."

Kim straightened and growled at the radio. "Bastards." All the innocents who had been slaughtered by terrorists the past couple of decades disturbed her. It was one of the reasons she'd wanted to work with codes in particular. By breaking them down, there was a chance she could stop violence before it happened.

Arabic and English sentences, written white on a black background, tumbled through her brain. What was she missing? It felt as if the key were just out of reach, just beyond her peripheral vision.

"Look to the middle of things," said a voice in her memory. It was the voice of her first mentor, Arthur Tsosie, a Navajo who had served the United States as a code breaker in World War II.

Arthur had been stable master at the Athena Academy where Kim had gone as a shy and awkward twelve-year-old. Lonely away from her big family, but also determined not to let on that she wasn't just as tough as the other girls, Kim had often retreated to the stables. Arthur, coming upon the bereft and weeping little girl who missed her family, had befriended her. The old man had provided a pocket of retreat for her when things had become too overwhelming.

And his stories of his adventures as a code talker, told in his lilting, soft tenor, had lit a passion in Kim that had never abated. When she proved to be gifted with both maths and languages, becoming a code breaker had been the obvious choice.

Arthur had always delivered his tidbits of knowledge while caring for the horses. Memories of him were now accompanied by scents of straw and dusty sunlight. She could see his hands, the color of pecans and gnarled into knots so the fingers looked like branches, grasping the currycomb as it moved through a pale blond mane. "The trick to seeing any-thin'," he'd say, "is to remember it's not what it is on the outside. Code, woman, friend, dog—it's all the same. Look through the top to the middl-a things."

Look through the top.

Often that meant simply letting go of perceptions as they stood, to allow new angles to enter her brain. Kim let the reams of code float over the surface of her closed eyelids. The e-mails were exchanged in Arabic, or at least in Arabic script. The messages had almost certainly begun in the Arabic language, as well, although the words were now nothing recognizable in any language the computers could read.

The quirky dots and swirls of Arabic lettering moved on her eyelids, a dance. Along with computers that had been running the cipher text through programs all day, Kim and her partner, Scott, had been manually trying various approaches to decipher the code.

The Arabic letters turned into a swirling, Jasmine-and-Aladdin cartoon script, the dots exaggerated. She slammed her feet to the floor, jolting herself back awake.

"Damn," she said. "Damn. Damn. Damn." A sense of urgency built in her chest.

Solve the code.

The answer was right there. She could feel it. What was she missing?

Kim focused on the computer screen and punched some buttons on her keyboard to bring up the program running in the background.

From the radio on her desk came a somber female voice. "President James Whitlow endured questions from the press today regarding the Tom King-Puerto Isla scandal. Many Americans are beginning to question the connection between Puerto Isla and the current unrest in Berzhaan."

To wake herself up, Kim said aloud, "Unrest in Berzhaan. There's an unusual situation."

The unrest wasn't unusual, but some blamed the United States, or at least the current administration, for the trouble in the small Middle Eastern country. It didn't matter to Kim whether the assessment was correct or incorrect—her concern was that there were terrorist cells that were determined to punish what they saw as the evil empire of the United States and make a statement by whatever means necessary.

With presidential elections coming up and the general unease about the world situation and the scandal of Puerto Isla hanging over the President, the situation offered too many opportunities.

Again she felt the urgency, that hollow sense of dread. *Break the code.*

On the radio, the announcer went on, "In other news, presidential candidate, Gabriel Monihan, appeared at a packed rally in New York City this afternoon, part of a ten-city election blitz that began yesterday in Washington, D.C."

A window on Kim's work computer popped up. In a blue box with red lettering, she read:

LEXLUTHOR: How's the code chopping?

Kim grinned. Alexander Tanner was an FBI bomb-squad expert in Chicago who had assisted her with a case two months ago, when a young hacker used bomb schematics to encrypt messages through the upper reaches of government. Privately, Kim had been impressed with the kid, a bored seventeen-year-old with too much time on his hands and a brain that needed challenges. Lex had been the first to spot the schematics while working an unrelated case and had e-mailed Kim to ask her advice over whether the coding could be done.

Their cooperation—an NSA employee and an FBI agent—would have been unheard of several years ago. Animosity had been more the game in those days. But reporter after reporter had turned up examples of situations that could have been defused by real communication between agencies and the pressure to cooperate had become too powerful to resist. The top-level security agencies in the country were—at least officially—encouraging interdepartmental communication, including this connected link of instant messaging within the various agencies.

It was working. Sort of. The animosity between various agencies, the secretive and jealous ways they guarded their sources, the eternal race to see who would solve which problem first, would never entirely disappear.

Although she'd never met Lex in person, Kim liked his sense of humor and his breezy ways—such as using the name of a comic-book supervillain as his instant-messaging handle.

She typed:

WINDTALKER2: Hey, guy! Still chopping. You're out late.

LEXLUTHOR: The same could be said of you.

WINDTALKER2: Trying to crack this baby. Feels big.

LEXLUTHOR: Yeah? Wanna brainstorm?

WINDTALKER2: Might be getting too scattered to think now. A.M.?

LEXLUTHOR: No can do. Big meetings.

Kim was overtaken by a yawn. She typed:

WINDTALKER 2: All right. How come you're working so late?

LEXLUTHOR: Politicians up the wazoo in Chicago this week. Green candidate today. Prez appearing tomorrow. Monihan on Thursday.

WINDTALKER2: Bomb scares?

LEXLUTHOR: Dozens. Every lunatic in the greater metro area has a plan for saving the world. Gotta check 'em all. Been over the courthouse twenty times. The airport at least 452.

WINDTALKER2: 452? That would take a little time.

LEXLUTHOR: Well, maybe it was only six times. FELT like 452.

WINDTALKER2: Any bombs anywhere?

LEXLUTHOR: Nope. Real bombers don't call ahead.

WINDTALKER2: Ah.

LEXLUTHOR: Hey. I looked up your picture on the company site.

WINDTALKER2: That's creepy, Luthor

LEXLUTHOR: Somebody told me you were hot.

WINDTALKER 2: It was probably me. I am not, and don't you forget it.

LEXLUTHOR: Kinda short. But then, I'm kinda ugly, so I guess we're even.

WINDTALKER2: Short is a state of mind.

LEXLUTHOR: <clearing throat delicately> I might be in your area next week. You up for a cup of coffee or something?

WINDTALKER2: Hold on.

LEXLUTHOR: What are you doing?

WINDTALKER2: Checking out YOUR picture. What if you're really ugly?

LEXLUTHOR: No fair going to the academy photo.

She opened a second window on the computer and ran a search for Alex Tanner, Federal Bureau of Investigation, Chicago, then clicked on the first link. Which was the Academy photo.

Kim grinned. It showed a serious-looking young man, about 21, skinny and with a nose almost too big for his face.

WINDTALKER2: <SNICKER>

LEXLUTHOR: Damn. I've put on a few pounds since then.

WINDTALKER2: Good thing.

LEXLUTHOR: We're all geeks at 21. Check this link
out: www.oaksidetelegraph.com/article00364.htm

WINDTALKER2: Yeah, yeah, Luthor. It's probably
a link to Heath Ledger.

But Kim clicked on the link, which took her to a
newspaper site, and a headline that read, "Bomb
Squadron Safety Record Vetted." Beneath it was a
photo of a man in a black T-shirt that showed off very
nice shoulders, a good chest and *excellent* arms.

Kim raised an eyebrow. His hair was cropped to
show a well-shaped head, high cheekbones and, yep,
that aggressive nose. Which was a lot sexier on a
thirtysomething face.

And he had that mouth, a Denzel Washington
mouth, with an overbite and a full lower lip that
looked very sexy.

Kim had a weakness for lips like that.

WINDTALKER2: Okay.

LEXLUTHOR: Okay, what?

WINDTALKER2: Okay you won't shame me. I'll
have coffee next week.

LEXLUTHOR: Not sure I can handle the exuber-
ance, babe.

WINDTALKER2: Babe? What century are you?

WINDTALKER2: Hang on....

WINDTALKER2: Something coming up on my de-cryption.

The computer was making a soft, double beep that meant something had been noted in a special file. When she opened it, she frowned.

WINDTALKER2: Hmm. Odd.

LEXLUTHOR: Que?

WINDTALKER2: It's an odd signature file.

LEXLUTHOR: Not my area, kiddo. I'll let you get to it.

WINDTALKER2: K-O.

LEXLUTHOR: Next week.

"What am I missing?" she asked herself, peering hard at the screen.

And if she didn't find the answer, who was going to die because of it?

A small musical noise told her an e-mail had arrived

in her personal in-box. It brought the total to twenty-eight, and Kim remembered she'd meant to check the box. Her eyes burned and she knew she needed to get to bed if she was to have any brain at all the next day, but her little sisters were always wounded if she didn't respond, so she dutifully opened the folder marked "Family."

"Shit!" she said aloud.

There were two messages from her mother. One was—Kim sighed—an e-mail hoax that had been around for years, about people flashing their headlights erroneously.

The other…

TO: kvalenti@rsme.net
FROM: eileenvalenti@dearbornhosp.org
SUBJECT: Sunday dinner
Hi, honey. I've been on the phone all day and the girls finally stole it from me. Don't forget, next Monday is the Columbus Day parade and your sisters' hearts will be broken if you don't show up to watch them tap dance on the police float. I was going to have our big meal that day, but nobody wanted to shift the tradition, so we'll just do it Sunday, as always. Try to come for both, huh? Bring a friend if you want. Maybe your big handsome partner??
Love,
Mom

Below the message from Eileen was a list of twenty-seven e-mails, repeated over and over down the length of the window. Each carried her sister Lynda's e-mail address, lyndavalenti2@rsme.net, and the same subject line: LOOK WHAT I FOUND ONLINE! A paper-clip icon sat beside each one.

"Lynda, Lynda, Lynda," Kim said, and opened her virus protection software to isolate and examine the virus. "How many times I gotta tell ya not to open attachments, kid?"

When the box was cleared, she examined the isolated virus. It turned out to be a relatively benign form that simply replicated and sent e-mails to every address on an account. Not such a big deal if the infected computer was the personal machine of a teenage girl, but costly and damaging if it was the mainframe of a big corporation.

The fact that she did have a teenage sister was one of the reasons Kim kept her e-mail accounts so rigidly separated.

She sent her sister a warning message with instructions to remove the infected files from her own computer. In capital letters, she typed:

DO NOT OPEN ATTACHMENTS. EVER. Love, Kim.

Something jiggled in her brain, right at the edge. The answer.
It was there, then gone, like a phantom.

"Get some sleep, Valenti," she said.
Without dreams.
Please.

Chapter 2

The following morning, Kim glared at the computer screen at work. They still had not made significant progress. Whatever clue was niggling at the edge of her brain had refused to come forth.

Her partner, Scott Shepherd, dropped down beside her, a sheaf of papers in his hands. "Anything?" he asked. His eyes looked as red as her own probably did, and she offered her bottle of eyedrops.

"That bad?"

"Three-day-bender bad."

"Real men don't use eyedrops. We just belt some

bourbon and make it look authentic." He rubbed his eyes. "The whole place needs new monitors, however. The refresh rate sucks."

Kim leaned back and pointed at the screen with the eraser end of a pencil she'd been chewing on. "What do you make of this signature file? It shows up on all of them, invisible in the e-mail itself, but running in the background."

He frowned at the screen, stroked his chin where he'd worn a goatee until joining the NSA. "I see it, but it's not bringing anything up for me right this second."

Rolling her tired shoulders, she stood. "I feel like we're so close. It's driving me crazy."

"I know."

She pushed her chair under the desk, smacked his arm. "C'mon. Let's get on the treadmills for a half hour, talk it out. Maybe there's something we're missing." She stretched the muscles of her back, hard.

"Sounds good." He dropped the papers on her desk. "I pulled these up. Maybe there's something else here."

"Last one on the treadmills is a rotten egg."

In the women's locker room, Kim stripped out of her day clothes, a straight blue skirt, white blouse, stockings and low-heeled pumps. It was great to shed the uniform for stretchy shorts, a sports bra with a T-shirt over it, her comfortable Nike running shoes. She tugged her dark hair into a scrunchie and tucked her earrings into her pocket.

Exercise would help clear the cobwebs. She tossed a towel over her shoulder and made her way into the fitness center.

There were few people around. Although the NSA worked around the clock, this was generally a lull period. Scott had claimed a treadmill in the empty line, and she took the one beside him. She punched in numbers to get to a moderate jog and found her pace, then said, "So what's going down? If you were a terrorist, what would you be targeting?"

He shook his head. His jaw was grim. "The elections are a possibility."

The presidential elections would be held in a few weeks, and there had been a great deal of controversy over the incumbent, President James Whitlow. "Who'd be the best target?"

"I'd kill the young, handsome one," he said.

Kim chuckled. "Personally dislike the guy, huh?"

"It's the tragedy factor—an old guy gets blown up, even if he's a president, it's not as big a deal as when a charming and handsome younger guy gets it."

"Good point." Kim nodded. "Then again, terrorists have little love for the president, and it's plain he's not particularly effective at home or abroad."

"Especially in Berzhaan."

"Right. All the more reason terrorists might target him. Or maybe to get people to vote the way they want them to, as with Spain and maybe this new Munich thing. Get them to vote for Monihan."

Scott made a derisive noise. "I'm still having trouble taking Monihan seriously."

Kim wiped a lock of hair out of her eyes. "What's the matter, Shepherd? He's prettier than you?"

"Nah. I'm serious here. He's too young, and the only reason he's so popular is because all these women are swooning over his pretty face."

"So, you've got to be old and ugly to be a good president?"

He shot her a grin. "Adds dignity."

Kim rolled her eyes. "And Whitlow is so dignified."

"He's a statesman of the old school, you gotta admit."

"Mmm. The who-cares-where-the-money-comes-from-as-long-as-I-get-elected school." Whitlow was suspected of accepting money from a drug lord in Puerto Isla, and worse, sending in a SEAL force, which was then demolished, to cover it up. "Whitlow's finished."

"Maybe. Unless they kill Monihan."

They ran in silence for a moment. Feet thumped rhythmically against the rubberized mats, and the motors whirred quietly. Kim felt her breath going deeper, expanding her lungs with oxygen—oxygen that then enlivened her brain cells.

"They're planning something big," Scott said grimly. "I feel it in my gut."

"Me, too. If we don't break this code, what are we going to find out in the worst way?"

"Exactly."

"It's a pretty sophisticated network," Kim said. "So we're looking at high-level planning."

"It'd be nice if terrorists were as stupid as criminals, but they wouldn't get far in the modern world."

She grinned.

They ran in companionable silence for a while. After a few minutes, Kim felt a click of endorphins, and the stress seemed to drain out of her body in a rush, as if someone had pulled a plug in her toe. "Ah," she said, and blew out hard. "Better."

She glanced at Scott, who had sweat pouring down his rugged, well-cut face. "Admit it," she said. "This feels pretty good."

"Yeah, Valenti, you're as smart as you are good-looking."

"Sweet-talker."

He blotted his face. "So they say."

"The secretarial pool swoons when you walk through, Shepherd, along with half the cryptographers." She gave him a sidelong grin. "Male and female."

"Why do you keep ribbing me about this, huh? I think you have a secret crush on me."

"That's true. And you know me, I'm so mild mannered, I can't come right out and say it."

He laughed. "Mild mannered. Yeah, right." He punched the controls. "Climb some hills?"

"You bet." She punched in the incline numbers and grinned. It was the reason she liked working out with him—he was extremely competitive and pushed her to better levels. The hills were a point of pride. He'd grown up in Colorado, in a little ski town, and boasted terrific lung capacity. Kim had gone to prep school in Arizona, running the scorching mountain paths around Phoenix, and boasted her own great lungs.

They'd been in some grim contests. "Six," she said, referring to the level of incline on the treadmill.

He nodded. They ran, breath coming too hard now for brainstorming or any other kind of conversation.

As her body sweated, her brain awakened, ran a thousand algorithms, trying to fit the pieces together. It wasn't exactly a one-two-three process, a conscious thing, but a running stream of numbers, letters, patterns.

"Seven," Scott said.

Kim punched the up arrow on the treadmill and leaned forward the slightest bit to accommodate the greater incline. The numbers and patterns kept whirring in her head. Once her brother Jason had asked her how she came up with the answers to number problems so fast, and she'd considered it seriously for a minute. The best analogy she could think of was a visual of a bike lock with spinning wheels. She just saw them, and they whirred until the right number appeared.

Her brain had always run patterns, looking for the ways things fit together. In the second grade, she'd been doing the newspaper Scramble every morning, and always got it right, even if she didn't necessarily know the word. By fourth grade, even her very traditional Italian father was forced to admit his daughter was something of a math whiz. They'd had to hire a tutor to keep up with her.

Her thighs started to burn the slightest bit, and her breath came harder. Next to her, Scott lifted an eyebrow. His athletic arms, bared by a serviceable gray tank, were shiny. "Eight," she said.

"Nine," he countered.

She didn't even bother to look at him, just pushed the arrow one more time. Sweat poured down her spine in a wash, and she wiped it off her forehead. Her feet clumped hard on the rubber matting, a fact she usually hated. Tonight, the sound was lost in the heavier pounding of Scott's tread.

The patterns whirred in her mind, and she stared into the middle distance, not seeing the white-painted cinder-block wall with its poster citing heart-rate targets, but a stream of code. Ordinarily, e-mails were a less difficult form of code to crack, because certain elements, such as headers and addresses, remained constant, and once the code could be cracked there, it fell wide open.

Not in this case. The agency had collected hundreds of e-mails over the past several weeks, as many as fifty in a single day, but in spite of their best efforts with computer algorithms and sophisticated code-breaking software, they'd made no headway.

"What…" Kim gasped, "are we…missing?"

"Network," he growled. "Some network angle."

Her breath was growing ragged, and her thighs were burning. She ran five to seven miles a day, as well as lifting weights and practicing kung fu for strength, but the hills were always killer. Licking salt from her upper lip, she slid a glance toward her partner to see how he was holding up.

Sweat soaked his shirt and his streaky blond hair, but Kim only needed that one glance to know he'd hit his stride. Back straight, breath heavy but even. It was easy to see him running up some forested mountain trail at ten thousand feet, his powerful body in perfect condition. Like an ad for a sport drink.

"Uncle," she said, and pushed the arrows to bring the incline down to a more normal level.

"Thank God," he said. "I thought it was going to be me this time."

"Damn," she said, and blew out a heavy breath. "One of these days, Shepherd. I am going to kick your high-altitude butt."

"Yeah, yeah, Valenti."

She wiped her face. As if the towel wiped away a

layer of confusion, the answer to the signature was suddenly plain.

"It's a virus," she said.

Chapter 3

Scott wiped his face with a towel. "*What* is a virus?"

"That's what the signature is, a virus mark. It's using the virus to encode the messages, the same way a virus works to infect computers."

"I'm not following."

"It's a lot more confusing to say it than it is in action. When you get a regular e-mail virus, it comes in through your e-mail program, right? Then goes out through the addresses in your address book."

"Okay." He lifted the towel to his mouth.

"This is working the same way. The guy writes his message, adds the signature line, and it goes through the e-mail systems, bouncing here and there and everywhere, gaining a layer of corruption—in this case, encryption—with each bounce."

"Jeez. So how do they decode it?"

"There's obviously a key at the other end."

A slow grin broke on his angled face. "Let's go find it."

It was the break they'd been looking for. Within twelve hours, Kim and Scott had broken down the e-mails and sorted them into two piles so that they could each run decryption possibilities.

The most logical place to look was the source of the virus itself. Most encryption was "private-key," that is, it used the same key to encrypt the message as would be used to decrypt it. While there was such a thing as "public-key" encryption, where the encoding key was different from the decoding key, it was very slow and would be too noticeable for an e-mail virus. By examining the virus, they were able to crack the code itself.

Which left another layer: the e-mails had been written in Arabic and had to be translated into English so the bulk of the messages could be read by the team.

Even then, there were missing pieces of information, but pointers clearly indicated there was trouble on the way. It looked as if it would be centered around Chicago.

"We've gotta call Dana," Kim said.

"You want me to make the call?" Scott asked.

Kim gave him a glare. "No way. He can be a bastard all he likes, but he can't stop me."

Scott lifted a shoulder. "Why subject yourself to such a jerk? He's old school, no point in banging your head against the wall."

"Because dealing with me means he learns, over and over, that women are in this organization to stay."

"Suit yourself." He waved a file. "I'll get this copied."

Despite her bravado, Kim had to brace herself before she picked up the phone. Dana Milosovich was a fifty-something CIA diehard, who thought women should be secretaries, whores or wives. Not operatives. Not code breakers. He had not forgiven Kim for an incident last spring, when she'd beaten him to the draw on an important case.

Too bad.

On the other end of the line, the phone rang. "Milosovich." His voice was as gravelly as five miles of bad road, no doubt from decades of smoking contraband Cuban cigars.

"Hello, Dana. It's Kim Valenti, from NSA. You have a minute?"

"A short one."

"Thanks for your graciousness."

"Don't mention it. What is it?"

"We've been following some suspicious e-mail activity related to the Q'rajn. My partner and I broke

the code this morning and it appears to be pointing
to plans for a terrorist attack in Chicago."

"Yeah?"

"Looks like a bomb. Maybe a truck, something to
do with the bridges over the river or a freighter on
the lake. They've created a virus code to encrypt the
e-mails, which we've broken, but on top of that, the
cell is using another layer of code substituting one
group of activities for another. We haven't entirely
sorted that part out, but we're pretty sure the site is
Chicago."

"We're way ahead of you, Valenti. Our operatives
have been following the same cell. They're Berzhaanian rebels, and were planning to stage an event
to draw attention to the situation in their county."

Kim scowled. "Right, but we—"

"Two key members of Q-group were killed in
Berzhaan yesterday. We feel certain they're no longer
an immediate threat, and in fact recommended
that Homeland Security step down to a level-yellow
alert."

"What were their names?"

"Whose names?"

Kim pressed the eraser end of a pencil into the
spot between her eyebrows. "The Berzhaanians who
were killed."

"Oh, let's see. Ahmed bin Hoshel and Sabrout Al
Javid El Thakur."

Not her guys, but she paused and double-checked

her notes before she spoke. No. Not the same names she had received from Oracle, but she couldn't reveal that source. "Hmm. They may very well have been leaders in Berzhaan, but the e-mails we've examined have all originated within the U.S. It's a different cell."

"You don't know that. They could have coded it from anywhere."

"Not exactly," Kim returned. Patiently, she thought. "There are ways to track addresses, but it's more a matter of a pattern of exchange. The IP addresses are American. It looks like it's out of the Chicago area somewhere, as well."

"Is that so." He coughed, a rattly, gray sound. "Don't know how to help you, missy."

"I'm asking you to check out the possibility of a terrorist attack in Chicago."

"It's done. The FBI has been over the city with a fine-tooth comb. Without a lot more information, I don't see why we need to be wasting more manhours and causing more unrest."

Kim could read between the lines: there was a lot riding on this election, and the incumbent Whitlow needed things to appear stable, even if they weren't. "Look, Milosovich, I know you don't like me, but how're you going to feel when a bunch of civilians get blown up because you want to piss in my cornflakes?"

"Give me something a little more substantial, and we'll get right on it, sister."

Scott came back, dropped a file on his desk opposite hers and raised an eyebrow. Kim rolled her eyes. "How about I give you names?"

"What names?"

"Two people associated with the terrorist cell we think is planning this attack on Chicago. They're based just outside of the city."

"Let me have 'em."

"Not without a guarantee that I can have some cooperation."

"What do you want?"

"Whatever you've got on these men."

A short pause. She heard him rattling something. Maybe a canister of pens. "All right. Let me have 'em."

With some reservations, Kim said, "Fathi bin Amin Mansour and Hafiz abu Malik Abd-Humam."

Milosovich broke into a ragged, wet chuckle. "That loser? Abd-Humam is running a tire store downtown. He's been here since his college days. Fathi Mansour...don't know him."

"My intelligence says he's a professor with no known terrorist ties. But we both know that doesn't mean anything."

"I'll look into it, see what we've got, but I wouldn't hold my breath. I'm telling you the cell was castrated when the leaders were killed in Berzhaan."

"Hope you're right."

"You know, Valenti, your arrogance pisses me off. I've been doing this since before you were born. You hotshot kids come in here with all your jargon and think you can save the world in five minutes flat, but it doesn't work like that."

Kim struggled with an array of answers, from the unprintable to the compassionate. He was an old man on his way out. He knew it and resented it. She could understand that, but not at the risk of human lives. "I'm sorry to have taken up so much of your time, Mr. Milosovich," she said finally. "You'll let me know if you turn anything up."

"You got lucky once, that's all," he said. "You broke a code."

"Well," she said slowly, her nostrils flaring, "if it was lucky, then it was three times, because that's the number of codes I've broken since I arrived at the Agency."

"Whatever."

"Great comeback. You know, I'm trying to be patient with you, respect what you have to teach me. But you have to respect my knowledge, as well. Computers are here to stay, and just because they scare you, and you've got your voice-mail password stuck to your desk and you don't know how to collect e-mail without somebody setting the program for you, don't take it out on me. I'm trying to *help* you!"

"I don't want your help."

"Fine. Whatever." Kim hung up and let go of a howl. "He drives me insane!"

Scott chuckled, stapling a sheaf of papers together. "Better call the FBI before he gets to them."

"I have a better idea." Kim opened the Instant Messenger box.

WINDTALKER2: Hey, Luthor, are you there?

No answer. After five minutes, Kim reluctantly picked up the phone. She dialed his desk directly, but an electronic voice answered and said simply that her party was away from his desk. "Damn." She punched in the key to be connected to a central number.

A woman answered. "Federal Bureau of Investigation, Margaret speaking."

"Hi, Margaret. Kim Valenti from the NSA here. Is Lex around anywhere?"

"Not at the moment. You want his voice mail?"

"No, thanks. I need to share some concerns I have over a possible terrorist alert in Chicago. Who'd be my best bet?"

"I think you're probably all right, Ms. Valenti. We just had a call from the CIA about the same thing."

"I'm sure you did," Kim said as evenly as possible. "All the same, I'll feel better if I talk to somebody on the bomb squad. Who else?"

"I can put you through to Agent O'Brien."

"Thanks."

"Hold please."

"O'Brien here," said a voice with the edge of a Spanish accent. The juxtaposition made Kim smile. She explained who she was and what her mission of the day was, but before she could finish, O'Brien interrupted her. "Right. I just took a call from the CIA, an agent Milosovich. He said your guys have been killed, so it's not a problem."

Kim rubbed her temple. "Not *my* guys. *His* guys. My cell is located somewhere in the Chicago area, and they're planning something big. That *is* a problem."

"With all due respect, Agent—"

"Valenti."

"With all due respect, Agent Valenti, we've been over the city like dogs the past couple of weeks, sniffing out every corner."

"He told you I'm high-strung and prone to exaggerate."

"Words to that effect."

"Right. Is Lex Tanner around?"

"Nope. They're at the airport, going over it one more time, double-checking security standards. It's unofficially code orange, but we don't want to alarm the public."

"Can you have him call me when he gets back?"

"Will do."

Kim was about to hang up when O'Brien said, "Hold up. Tanner just got here. I'll put you through."

"Thanks."

She listened to the sound of Vivaldi piped through the lines for a minute, then a man said, "Tanner here. What can I do for you?"

Kim had never had a phone conversation with

him. All their business had been conducted via instant messaging or e-mail. For five-tenths of a second, she was startled by the unexpected richness of his voice. Humid with the blurred edges of somewhere south. *Deep* South.

"Hello?" he repeated.

"Hey, Lex Luthor," she said, recovering. "Kim Valenti, at the NSA. How're you doing?"

"Darlin'!" The genuine pleasure in his voice was unmistakable. "I'm doing just fine now that I'm talking to you. What's up?"

"I've got a problem. Hoping you can help."

"I'll do my best."

"We have intelligence that shows a Q'rajn cell in the burbs of Chicago, and they're utilizing a virus to encode their e-mails. We broke the code and my partner and I are pretty sure they're targeting Chicago in some way."

"Yeah, well—"

"Damn it!" Kim swore. "Not you, too."

"Hold on. No need to get ugly, now. I just heard from your buddy at the CIA who said they caught your guys."

Gritting her teeth, Kim said, "First thing you need to know is that Milosovich is so not my buddy. He'd love to see me fall face-first in a mud puddle. Second, they're not my guys. They're Milosovich's guys, and he wants to think my guys were castrated by the fall."

"And you don't think they were."

"No. Those guys were in Berzhaan and they're undoubtedly all part of the same twisted terrorist sect, but my group is here, on American soil."

"All right. What's your intelligence say they're going to do?"

"It's not that clear. A bomb. Maybe the airport or an airplane."

"We've been over the airport five thousand times."

"I know. Believe me, I wouldn't insist if I weren't pretty sure."

He sighed. "Valenti, my hands are tied, babe."

"Don't call me that."

"Sorry. Old habit." She could hear a tapping sound, fast and tinny. "Look, it sounds like Milo-sovich and you have some bad blood, all right, but he's a good agent. And he's got a lot of seniority."

"And I don't."

"Exactly."

"Okay. Look, what if it's *not* the airport? What if it's along the route to the airport, or somewhere one of the candidates is going to speak? Bridges, television stations—" She paused, trying to brainstorm. "Wherever. You know your city."

He said, "Hmm." And in spite of her concern and irritation, she felt it on the back of her neck. Velvety, rich. "A question—why target the candidates anyway?"

"Because they can? Because it causes trouble?

Terrorists don't need a clearly defined reason to do things—they just want to create fear and confusion."

"I see your point." Again that background noise of quick tapping.

Kim said, "What is that noise?"

"Sorry." The sound ceased. "I have a bad habit of tapping a pen."

"No big deal."

"Look, Valenti, you've done me favors, and I'll see what I can do, all right? But maybe you oughta look at the intelligence in another way, too. Maybe it's not pointing where you think it is—and that would be tragic, too."

"You're right. I'll go over it again. Let me know what you find out."

"Will do." He dropped his voice, and his next words were even richer, darker, like chocolate. Laced with espresso. "We still on for next week in your neighborhood?"

"I've gotta tell you, Lex, your voice didn't hurt the cause any."

"Yeah? You like it?"

Kim smiled. "Call me if you find anything, Luthor."

"I'll be talking to you."

Scott, sitting at his desk, raised his head when she hung up. "You've got that gleam in your eye, Valenti."

"Don't be ridiculous," she said, and stood up. "I'm going to take some personal time. I'll be back later."

Chapter 4

She drove home and without taking off her coat, she fired off an e-mail.

To: Delphi@orcl.org
From: Ariadne@orcl.org
Subject: need help
Give me everything you have on Chicago, the campaigns, anything the Chicago set might have done previously. Not making a lot of progress through usual channels. Advise.
Ariadne

Still wearing her coat, she went to the kitchen, opened a vacuum-packed envelope of tuna and ate it

leaning on the counter. From the other room came a
soft beep and she walked back.

To: Ariadne@orcl.org
From: Delphi@orcl.org
Subject: re:
-Intelligence from CIA shows infiltration at Chic-
ago UBC television station, CIA might have a man
in there.
-Three moving vans were stolen last week in south-
ern California. Home-move type, not professional.
-Quote keeps showing up in unrelated material:
Good women are obedient. They guard their
unseen parts because Allah has guarded them.
Surah 4:34
-Reference to Cristopho in materials CIA inter-
cepted. Columbus? Clue to city or holiday? Check.
As always, act independently if necessary. Oracle
will back you.
Delphi

Kim narrowed her eyes, punched in a thanks. A
man at the Chicago UBC affiliate—at least it was a
place to start. Her gut was screaming that Chicago
was the place, the time not far distant. Not even as
far away as Columbus Day, which was Monday, either. The flurry of e-mails was so intense, the deal
had to be going down soon.

And if she couldn't figure it out, somebody would

die. Kim intended to do whatever was necessary to prevent that.

She picked up the phone, punched in some numbers. "Shepherd," she said when Scott answered, "I'm going to Chicago. Let the boss know for me."

"Whatcha got?"

"A hunch more than anything else. Not a lot more. Can you cover for me for a day or two?"

"I don't like it when you do the maverick thing, Valenti. Too nerve-racking."

"I know. But it's the way I was trained."

"This doesn't have anything to do with an FBI agent named Tanner, does it?"

"No. Why?"

"He left a message."

"Yeah?"

"Yeah."

Kim made a noise of annoyance. "Are you gonna tell me what it is?"

"'Checked it all. Everything is A-okay. Don't worry.'"

A ripple of something she didn't stop to identify raced through her—a twitchy mix of longing and regret. He hadn't taken her seriously, either, and it was far more disappointing coming from him. Her sharp response was a warning.

She'd do well to leave the man alone. Completely.

"Nope," she said. "Tanner is as clueless as all the

rest of them. You're the only one who ever believes in me. This trip is to check out a gut-level idea."

"Your mysterious source." Scott tsked. It wasn't the first time she'd received information through Oracle. She simply let him think whatever he thought about it. "All right, Valenti, I'll cover for you, but you keep that pretty ass out of trouble, will ya?"

"I'll do my best. If you need me, I'll have my cell phone with me."

"Stay in touch."

When she hung up with him, she looked up the number of the Chicago UBC station and called to speak with the personnel manager, a man named John. She identified herself as a member of the NSA, and said she was tracking some information regarding a case—would she be able to check the files tonight? He agreed warmly, said he'd be in that evening to train a new cameraman, and she could stop in at her convenience.

She changed into jeans and warm boots, but left her hair in a knot at the base of her neck. Into a small duffel, she threw a change of clothes and her makeup bag. From a rack on the back of her closet door, she chose a small shoulder purse, and tucked in her wallet, cell phone, and at the last minute, her NSA security badge. Within an hour, she was at the airport.

The ticket had been purchased at the last minute, so Kim wasn't surprised when she was pulled out of the security lines for additional screening—and not just the usual, extra hand-wanding, but a full, focused search of her belongings and the body search by an appropriate female guard. The girl was skinny as a praying mantis, her elbows like knots. Her blond hair was tightly pulled back from her extremely young—and serious—face.

Kim joked, "All clear? For once, I remembered to not wear an underwire bra."

"Wait right here." The girl picked up a phone, punched in a number.

Scowling Kim said "What is—"

"Better if you just follow directions, ma'am." She turned away and said something into the phone, looking at the NSA badge with Kim's picture.

Kim felt passersby giving her the curious eye. Odd how it made her feel guilty.

"I'm afraid there's an additional problem, ma'am," the girl said. "You'll have to follow me, please."

"Sure, but—"

"High alert this week and you have a lot of red flags."

"Last-minute ticket, I know. It's just that I work for—"

The woman flashed Kim's confiscated badge. "National Security Agency. I know."

Kim scowled at the rudeness and rolled her eyes. She looked younger than she was, she knew that. No point in antagonizing the woman further—it would just lead to more delays. "Will this take long? I'm worried about missing my flight."

"There's another one at 3 p.m. if you miss this one," the woman said without looking at Kim.

"Great." It wasn't. It would mean getting to Chicago after dark, maybe not to the television station until the evening news. With an effort, she breathed in. Out. No point in getting upset. It wouldn't hurry anything.

At an office with a window overlooking the concourse, the woman stopped and shoved open the door. "Here we are. Have a seat, ma'am."

A tall, bearded black man in a Transportation Security Administration uniform waved Kim into the chair. The woman escort handed over Kim's bags and badge, then exited.

"I'm sorry about the delay," the man said. "I need to verify your identity."

"No big deal."

As the man dialed the telephone, Kim fidgeted, irritably wiggling her foot until she realized it would make her appear to be nervous. Which she was, though not because she wanted to blow up the airport.

The airport. Why had the FBI in Chicago paid so much attention to the airport? Airports were so heavily guarded since 9/11 that there had to be an easier way for a terrorist to accomplish goals of instilling fear. Why bother? Narrowing her eyes in thought, Kim decided the FBI must have had some intelligence they weren't sharing.

The man hung up the phone. "I'm afraid we have to hold you for twenty minutes, just until they can fax a photo to your boss."

"I'll miss my flight."

"Sorry, ma'am. When it goes to orange, it gets a lot tighter around here."

Tamping down her annoyance, Kim folded her hands around her knees. "I appreciate that, but I'm bewildered. Why the trouble today? I've flown a dozen times under similar circumstances recently."

"I'm not at liberty to say."

"If I get through the security clearance will you tell me?"

He nodded. "That'd be all right, I guess."

The fax went through with a series of beeps and bleeps. Kim stared through the window over the concourse at the streams of humanity bustling through the hallways. She puzzled over the challenge of clearing millions and millions of passengers every day. Millions.

And it wasn't as if criminals hadn't proven they were willing to do anything to reach their objectives. Q'rajn wanted to punish the U.S. for its involvement in Berzhaan. Other rebels wanted other things, and anyone with an ax to grind, a pound or two of plastic explosives and a death wish could do it. For terrorists of the ilk they were all trying to fight, life was as thin and cheap as paper.

Watching the crowds, she tried to imagine she

was the one trying to decide who was a terrorist and who was an ordinary citizen. A tall man in a business suit looked like a physician, hurrying toward an important surgery. The turban on his head marked him as a Sikh, something Kim knew from her studies at Athena Academy. Exotic, but likely not dangerous.

But how would the ill-educated girl who'd carted Kim up here know that?

Odd, but sitting in the plastic chair in the office of the head of security made Kim *feel* guilty.

"It's a pretty rough job, the security of airports," she offered.

The man, his hands steepled in front of his mouth, raised weary brows. "That's understating the situation, I'd say."

"It's impossible, really, isn't it?"

He shook his head. "Never give up." The fax machine spit out a piece of paper and the man leaned forward to swipe it off the tray. "Looks like you're good to go, Ms. Valenti. Sorry for the delay."

Kim shrugged and took the things he held out to her. "So, I assume it was the late booking that caused so much trouble, but what else? I'll try to avoid it next time."

He scratched his nose. "Not sure you'll be able to do anything about it. The girl—er—thought you looked Arabic."

"Ah." She met his eyes.

He held her gaze for a second, then lifted a phone. "I'll call your gate to have them hold your flight."

Kim hitched the bag over her shoulder. "Thanks."

On the concourse, she headed for her gate, glancing up over her shoulder at the two-way window. Something niggled—there was something they weren't telling her. What could it be? What information had gone out that she'd not yet seen?

As she walked, she took the cell out of her bag and punched in the numbers to Scott's desk. The phone rang at the other end as she reached the deserted gate.

An impatient flight attendant stood irritably at the door to the flight. Kim handed the woman her boarding pass. "Sorry. Got stuck at security."

"Not your fault." The woman gave her back the small piece of pass. "Have a good flight."

Scott's voice mail picked up. "Shepherd," Kim said, hurrying down the ramp, "run the files again and see if there are any references to women, then get back to me. I'm getting on the plane right now, so I have to turn off my phone, but leave a message."

Chapter 5

By the time she dropped her bag on the bed in her Chicago hotel room, Kim was famished, grumpy and grimy. After a quick shower, she tucked her badge into her purse, bought a sandwich from the small deli in the hotel lobby and sat down to eat it with a cup of coffee by the windows.

She bit into the sandwich and took a single moment to appreciate it. A fantastic Reuben, layered with film-thin pieces of corned beef, fresh, crispy sauerkraut, melted Swiss cheese and just a smear of thousand-island dressing. Some things in life were worth appreciating. A great sandwich after a long day was one of them. The coffee, she discovered, was excellent, too.

Right after Jason was killed, Kim had gone through a period of dullness, where the world had felt as if it were a long way away from her. None of it had sharp corners or bright colors or any real detail, as if she were viewing it all through watery glasses. Everything was muted, turned down— sounds, sights, tastes, feelings.

One night, she had a dream that her brother slapped her. "Wake up!" he cried in the dream. "It's all right there, everything I can't have."

And she spent the next days in agony, finally beginning to feel by first acknowledging that her brother was never coming home. She owed it to him to be alert and aware of life—eating a sandwich, dancing, making love. Whatever.

As she ate, watching snow drift slowly, lightly from the dark sky, she turned her cell phone back on and checked for messages. There were two.

One was from Lex Tanner: "Valenti, I got this number from your partner." Kim bent her head, hiding a smile over the pleasure of hearing his voice again. That honeyed, rich drawl! "Sorry about earlier. Don't hold it against me, huh?"

She moved to the next message, which was from Scott. "Hey, I got the information you wanted. There's only one reference to women, a quote from the Koran," he said. "'Good women are obedient. They guard their unseen parts because Allah has guarded them. Surah 4:34.'"

Kim frowned. The same quote Delphi had sent her. *Women, unseen parts…* She narrowed her eyes, waiting for something to click. How would they use women? Considering the general attitude of Q'rajn, a conservative Muslim group, Kim didn't see them using women as warriors.

Still, it was another piece of the puzzle. Too bad she didn't know where it fit.

She finished her sandwich and tossed the cup and napkin into a trash bin, then headed out. She had other hunches to check out tonight. Maybe something at the television station would help the quotation make sense.

It was a cold, blustery evening. An icy wind blew off the lake, carrying a threat of snow. Kim huddled into her coat and wished for a warmer hat.

Winter. Ugh. With a swift sense of longing, she remembered the Arizona desert, clear and bright through the winter. It could be quite cold at times, but the air was never heavy, and what snow fell would be gone the minute the sun came out.

Not like winter in the East and Midwest, where the wind was bitter and the snow could lie on the ground for months, gaining layer after layer after layer of grime and disgustingness. She should have brought a warmer coat.

Tucking her chin closer, she hailed a cab to take her to the UBC station. The cabbie, a large-eyed man with an Iranian accent, said, "Terrible night out, isn't it?"

Kim shivered. "I hate this weather."

"Do you mind if I listen to the news on the radio?" he asked, his dark hand on the radio dials.

"Not at all." She leaned back and let the headlines wash over her. As they crossed a bridge over the river, she admired the shimmer of light on the water, the tall buildings stretching up toward heavy clouds.

"Several protestors refused to disperse and were arrested this afternoon in front of President Whitlow's campaign headquarters," said a sober male voice. "Approximately one hundred activists gathered to voice disapproval of rumored U.S. involvement in Berzhaan politics."

Kim rubbed a spot between her eyes. Would the terrorists target a demonstration? It was certainly a place to kill and wound a lot of people. Would there be others this week? She made a mental note to check which special interest groups were most vocal in the Windy City, and see if they'd been granted permission to demonstrate.

"Presidential candidate Gabe Monihan is expected to raise large crowds in Chicago tomorrow. The popular candidate will speak at 10 a.m. tomorrow at Loyola University. Traffic along the route is expected to be extremely heavy."

The taxi driver snorted. "That means it will not move," he said.

Kim chuckled 'I'm sure."

The television station appeared to be very quiet, which Kim supposed was not surprising, considering it was nearly 9 p.m. It seemed odd to find it so empty after the high security at the airport. If Kim was a terrorist, she'd pick news venues every time, but she couldn't think of a single staging in a news station ever, in any country.

Hmm.

She paid the driver, hitched her duffel over her shoulder and went inside. A single woman sat in a bulletproof cubicle that seemed absurdly well lit in the dim quiet of the waiting room just beyond. She pressed a button and asked Kim, "May I help you?"

She flashed her NSA badge. "I called a couple of hours ago. I'm meeting John from Personnel."

"Right. Just one minute." The girl picked up the phone and spoke into it. She put it down and pushed a buzzer. "Go through the double doors at the end of the hallway and John will meet you."

Kim found herself in a long hallway, hushed and empty. Discreet spots cast a thick amber light that left pyramids of shadow along the path.

She paused, struck by a sense of extreme uneasiness. The hair along the back of her arms rose the slightest bit. It was like the low growl of a dog who heard something before the humans in his realm— she stopped and listened carefully.

What was causing her discomfort? A sound just out of range? A scent that shouldn't be there? Something more primeval? Her training had taught her to respect such ripples of warning.

She listened intently. The low rush of air blowing through furnace vents, a slight, faraway humming that sounded more or less electronic. Nothing else. It was a television station, after all. The walls had to be soundproofed.

The only scents were the slightly chemical odors of carpeting and glue and other industrial materials, the faint dustiness of forced-air heat, her own hair releasing a ghost of damp lemony conditioner.

Nothing.

Something.

She turned in a circle. Maybe it was just the shape and depth of the shadows, the extreme stillness.

The bang of swinging doors sent a jolt through her, and she forced herself not to show it.

"Ms. Valenti!" said a man coming through the doors at the far end of the hallway. He looked oddly out of place in his Dockers and pale orange button-down shirt, as if someone had cut him out of an ad in a Seattle newspaper and pasted him into the wrong background. The haircut, the glasses, even his body language were too casual for this area. "I'm John Hallam," he said, extending his hand. "I'm afraid I don't have much time to talk to you—we thought you'd be here much earlier."

"My apologies," Kim replied "But I—"

"Right this way."

His handshake was cool and strong, in contrast to his youth, but she picked up a distinct sense of nervousness. "Thanks," she said. "Do you mind if I ask you a few questions?"

"Let's do that in the office, shall we?" He gestured for her to proceed ahead of him through the doors, and Kim stepped into a dark, open space crisscrossed with wires and cords and hulking shadows of equipment she didn't recognize. The ceiling stretched high into an area of steel girders, and Kim saw light shining from over a wall. Faintly, she heard voices.

At a second door, John paused. "They're about to go live for the news, but we have a few minutes. I thought you might want to meet some of the anchors." He smiled. "People generally do."

What could she say? *Not me?* So she smiled and shook hands with a trio of toothy, small, ultraclean people, noticing the facade of desk and backdrop against the cavernous, overarching darkness stretching above. Unease made her look around again.

Nothing. A cameraman fiddled with knobs on his machine. A bank of monitors showed six different screen shots. One was animated—she assumed it was the actual broadcast stream.

"Have any of you had threats or any reason to suspect trouble with anyone on the set?" she asked suddenly.

"No!" The young woman's eyes flew open. "John, is there a problem? Should we have guards again?"

"Again?" Kim echoed.

"Last summer—" the blonde began.

"One minute!" cried a stagehand or whatever he was called, a man with a thick beard and liquid eyes, rushing through with jeans and a loosely flapping shirt. He looked more like Chicago, Kim thought distractedly. Mixed race. Ethnic, anyway.

"John!" the blonde prompted, even as she straightened the front of her red suit and adjusted her mike.

"We'll talk about it later, Amber." John grabbed Kim's arm and hustled her toward another set of doors on the other side of the set. His hand settled at the small of her back, a firm pressure propelling her out of the room.

The hackles rose on her neck as they stepped through the doors. Kim instinctively took stock of her surroundings, noting exits—few—ceilings—high—windows—zero. It was like a fortress. It was curiously empty, as well. She would have imagined a television station to be a bustling, busy place, full of minions running around.

"Is it always so quiet around here?"

"Usually," John said. "The nuts and bolts of television are pretty straightforward—you need a good crew, but not a large one particularly." He opened a door halfway down a quiet corridor and waved her in ahead of him. "This is where we keep the personnel files."

He flicked on the overhead light, and cool green neon flooded the room. There were no windows, only a low ceiling of acoustic tile. The

walls were white, with a pair of motivational post-
ers. The carpet was industrial brown and orange,
endlessly forgiving and impossibly boring. A
bank of television screens ran down one end, and
John turned them on. They showed a series of
different shots—a commercial frozen in place, a
public-service announcement screen, and a logo
for UBC. The last showed a live feed of the anchors they'd just left.

"If you want to spread out on the tables, you're
welcome to do it." John unlocked the file cabinet
closest to the door and swung open a drawer. "I've
got to get back out there, but you should be able to
find whatever you need right here. New-hires to the
front, the rest alphabetized."

"Thanks."

"If you need anything, just dial 0 on that phone,
and you'll get the receptionist. She'll find me."

"Got it," Kim said, and frowned as she looked
around. The sense of things being a little off-kilter
still hung at the back of her neck. She disliked the
setup of the room at the end of a corridor, the lack
of exits, the grim lighting. Maybe it was just the fact
that there were no windows.

John still hung by the door, peering intently at one
of the screens. Kim saw there were dots of perspira-
tion on his top lip. "Big night, huh?" she ventured.

"What? Oh. Yeah, we have a new cameraman.
I'm worried about it."

"Go to it, then. I'll be fine."

He frowned at the screen, hurried out without answer. Kim looked at the bank of pictures to see what had bothered him, but nothing much seemed to have changed. Still the same three static pictures and the live feed of the news team. The woman was laughing as they made a switch, and suddenly a commercial blared into the room.

Kim winced and raced over to see if she could turn it down. There were several knobs and buttons and she experimented until she found the right one, turned it low, but not off. To avoid a repeat she found the same buttons below each of the screens and turned each one down.

Still feeling uneasy, she went to the door and stepped into the hallway. There was an exit sign about five hundred feet down the corridor. At least she knew how to get out if she had to. Moving her head on a neck still prickling and somewhat stiff, she listened in the hallway, but there was no sound.

Going back into the office, she tugged open the drawer and started looking through the files, one at a time. Each one contained background information, a résumé if one had been submitted, photos obviously taken in the same spot with the same camera for some kind of station ID and whatever notes anyone had made on them. There were seven new-hires dating back one year. None appeared to be out of the ordinary. Two cameramen, including the one John was fretting over tonight, a nervous-looking redhead with freckles head to toe and big golden eyes. A fifty-five-year-old woman hired to do secretarial work, who looked far younger than her age. Three support staff for the dining room.

John himself.

"Interesting," she said aloud, and flipped through his file. He'd been hired five months ago to take the place of the former station manager. An impeccable pedigree: a navy brat who had attended UCLA, done his time in the trenches as a reporter, and then drifted to the managerial side of the line. He'd come to Chicago via Florida.

A soft, almost subvocal whispering had been nagging her for several moments before she realized it. Kim lifted her head, frowning, and looked at the television screens. The news was back on, and it must be a sober story indeed, because the cheerleader was looking pretty grim. The camera angle was odd, too, and Kim shook her head. The cameraman was going to be in trouble.

Something wasn't quite right. She frowned and looked at the screens again. The whispering continued, but Kim could see nothing to account for it. The blonde was reading the news. The commercials stayed frozen.

Then the sibilant whispering sank in. She jerked up her head. A single word of the whisper penetrated suddenly—the Arabic word for woman. Her head jerked up and she stared at the television screens, listening intently. The lyrical rise and fall of the language was unmistakable, even in whispers, but she couldn't quite catch any other distinct words.

She peered at the screens. Where was it coming from? Moving to the bank of screens on the wall, she turned up the volume beneath each one. Silence greeted her on the first three. On the fourth, she heard a nonnative speaker brutalizing Arabic with harsh accents and dropped rolls. Maybe American, maybe German. Kim frowned and put her head down, listening closely. American. A man.

Two men spoke in quiet, hurried Arabic.

"We only have two choices," the first—nonnative speaker—said. "Monihan will be at the airport and we can take care of that then. We only have to secure the station until Mustafa accomplishes his mission at the airport."

"Her mission," snickered a second voice, this one a native Arabic speaker.

Her mission. Kim glanced at her watch. Two hours till the plane arrived at the Chicago airport. What was happening then? What did they have planned? It seemed an odd time for a bombing if a terrorist wanted to take out as many people as possible. She strained to hear what else the second speaker said, but the voice was softer, more liquid, and Kim couldn't hear it.

She raised her head. Where was the mike that was picking up the conversation? She glanced at the monitor, trying to tell if there were labels of any kind to guide her if she went back to the other room. The main screen said Camera One, predictably. Not much help. She'd have to take her chances.

From the set came a scream, and Kim jerked her attention back to the first screen. As she watched in horror, the set flooded with men who carried guns, running in what almost looked like formation. Quickly, she tried to count them: maybe five? Six?

From the midst of them came a dramatically tall and elegant man, obviously the head honcho. Kim recognized him immediately: Fathi bin Amin Mansour, the prodigiously intelligent Berzhaanian with degrees from Oxford. The man whose brothers and mother had been killed by Keminis four years ago. The man who was connected to several bombings.

The man she had been worried about leading a terrorist cell in Chicago.

He headed imperiously for the news desk, where the anchors cowered, stunned. One of the foot soldiers yanked the blond woman out of her chair on the set and shoved her roughly aside. She screamed, and her hands flew up protectively around her face, but another soldier simply shoved her to one side, out of sight of the camera.

"Damn," Kim whispered.

Mansour settled himself in the center chair and gestured with one long-fingered hand at the camera, which came closer and focused in on a face that would have been handsome without the light of fanaticism burning in his eyes.

In crisp, British-accented English, he said, "We have overtaken this television station on behalf of the people of Berzhaan, to protest the American involvement in our country's affairs. We have footage to show that the CIA has been involved in arms sales to the Kemini rebels, in order to keep our country in a state of unrest." He cued someone in the room, and a fuzzy video began to play.

Kim ceased listening and ran to the doorway and closed the door silently, turning off the light. Little chance they didn't know she was there, since it had only been ten minutes since she'd sashayed across the set. They'd come after her, but maybe she could figure something out in a minute or two. She tucked her hair under her collar.

On-screen, Mansour continued to talk, listing demands. A camera shot spun around and showed a line of station employees sitting in terror at one side of the set. A dark man with Arabic features stood over them, his face impassive, an assault weapon held loosely in his hands.

Behind them yawned the darkness of the cavernous studio. Kim glimpsed a man with a curiously expressionless face—this must the nonnative Arabic speaker—headed for a set of doors. With a jolt, she realized it was the doors toward the hallway that led to this office.

He was coming for her. And he didn't look as if he'd mind breaking a neck or a head or anything else.

Kim poked her head into the hallway, trying to gauge whether she had time to make it to the exit. But even as she stuck her head out, she heard the doors to the studio swoosh open. She dived back into the office, where at least the darkness could lend some surprise.

Through the crack, she could see down the hallway. He was a tall man with a shaved head and hardlooking eyes. He wore combat boots, and a desert camouflage shirt, and Kim wondered if he was military in some way. There was something wrong with his face, but she couldn't quite pin down what.

She had no doubt he was headed for this office and her. She looked around for a weapon and prepared to take him down.

Chapter 6

With the light off and the door closed, Kim had at least a small advantage. She found a flashlight on top of a filing cabinet and tested it for heft and swing, then took a spot by the door. Poised. When he came through the door, she'd knock him down and make a run for the back exit.

The door opened slowly. Kim heard her heartbeat in her ears, and her breathing was too loud. She tried to make it more shallow, tried to imagine he was a horse, trying to find her by scent and sound, and raised the flashlight over her head. As he came into the room, she began to swing it downward.

The man anticipated her move and caught Kim's

wrist before she could bring the full weight of the flashlight onto his head. The grab was awkward but fierce. Kim centered herself in a split second and used her body weight to pull him off balance. Swinging her elbow hard in an arc, she whirled and managed to yank her arm free.

He flipped sideways and countered with a body slam, hurtling her into the wall behind her. Air whooshed out of her lungs and her shoulder took a hard blow from a picture frame. She shoved him, gaining enough space to lift her elbow and shove it into his solar plexus. She ducked down and started to spin away—

But not quite fast enough. The man whirled with her and caught a thick handful of hair. He yanked upward and Kim found her body airborne, with nothing to grab except his arms, and she clung there as hard as she could, but he was much larger. With what seemed to be little effort, he slammed her downward into the conference table. Her cheekbone smashed into the wood, and for a moment, she was stunned. He grabbed her throat with both hands.

Kim gasped and with a sharp gesture flung her hands upward between his, then slammed her arms against the insides of his. His grip on her throat was broken, and Kim turned to scramble away, but he slammed her head against the table again, and she felt something cut into her upper ear with a vicious bite.

With a roar, she kicked backward, connected with what seemed to be his hip or upper leg, but there was no purchase on the slippery wood of the conference table. Before she could get away, he'd grabbed her hair, and slammed her face down again. Her lip and tooth hit the edge of the table and she tasted hot blood.

With a rebel cry, Kim kicked again, holding on to his arms to keep him off balance. Her left heel connected with his knee, and she kicked again, this time catching him in the gut, sending him off center enough that she could slide in his grasp, turn over on her belly and scramble across the polished surface of the table. He grabbed her foot. She kicked with the other and felt—heard—her heel crack against bone. Nose? Cheekbone? Chin?

"Bitch!" He grabbed her again, one hand around her neck, the other on her arm. She slid like a skater across the table. His hand scratched her neck. If he managed to get a hold on her in this position, there would be little she could do to keep him from strangling her to death.

With a cry, she turned toward him, catching him off guard enough that she could rear backward and, bracing herself with his arms, she slammed her forehead into his face. Something in her eyebrow gave as she connected with his jaw.

It knocked him, hard, and she did it again, slammed her forehead as hard as she could into his face. She hurt him. With a low guttural grunt, he let her go, and she stumbled backward.

It gave her a second to spring free. She bolted for the door.

Footsteps and voices in the hallway made her swing back toward the table, leaping instinctively for the top of the table, then to the file cabinets she'd been working from. No Expression was behind her, recovered, grabbing her ankle. She kicked at him and at the same time, banged a fist into the acoustic tile overhead and sucked in a breath when it flew out of its grid.

With a single, hard leap, she scrambled into the opening, disappearing into the dark. The man caught her ankle, but she kicked free.

Arabic exploded into the room as she pulled herself out of sight into the space above the ceiling. A bullet pinged through the tile to the right of her body, and she swore silently. She'd have to move.

It was very dark, and the gridwork felt unsteady, swinging faintly under her weight. Kim braced herself and prayed the whole thing didn't come down. If she stepped wrong, she'd put her foot through the ceiling tiles. The good thing was that none of her pursuers could follow her—the whole ceiling would come down. It was very dark. She gripped a single girder and inched along the length of it, feeling for the dividing wall she knew would have to be there. As silently as possible, she made her way through the darkness, feeling her way with feet and hands. Spiderwebs brushed her face. Light glowed over a wall to her left and she made her way toward it.

Two more bullets shattered the tiles behind her. One struck something close by and plaster dust scattered down on her. She winced instinctively. The movement made the metal beneath her foot give dangerously. Kim prayed that the metal would hold, that she was at least over another set of offices or in the hall.

A bullet whizzed through the air at her back. Shedding caution for speed, she hauled herself through the darkness, swinging from one set of girders to another.

She made it to what she assumed was the edge of the cavernous sets on the other side of the news desk. Crouching against a concrete support wall for a minute, she tried to get her bearings. Her eyes were adjusting to the dimness. Spears of light from bullet holes shot through the darkness, illuminating more than seemed possible.

She listened intently. The droning voice of the Arab at the news desk continued on, explaining terms and conditions of the hostages' release. No other voices. No more bullets.

Easing to a standing position, she peered over the wall and saw the loafered foot of a male hostage. The pale khaki sock pierced her. She imagined him putting it on this morning in his ordinary, carpeted bedroom, thinking it was going to be an ordinary work-day. She wondered if he had a child, or a wife who was waiting for him at home, her heart in her throat as the news of the hostage situation came in.

There was something trickling down her neck, and Kim put a hand up to wipe it away. Her sleeve came away smeared with blood. She swore. The ear hurt, but the blood was going to make it tough to look normal when she tried to get into a Chicago FBI sta-tion without the ID that was lying in her pack back in the conference room.

No help for it. She had to get out.

It was impossible to know exactly what was planned for the airport, but if Kim didn't get over there and at least try to figure it out, people would die. This diversion was meant to draw attention away from the planned bombing at the airport. If she didn't get out of here, warn someone, a bomb would blow up a presidential candidate and anyone who hap-pened to be in his realm. She wasn't going to let that happen.

Against her right breast, her cell phone suddenly buzzed. She slammed a palm over it, trying to muf-fle the sound, but the noise burst out of her jean-jacket pocket like a beacon to the shooters below.

Without taking time to silence the phone, Kim leaped for a girder, and grabbed on, swinging her body around and up. There was just enough light re-flected from the open room that she could make her way along the girder toward what she hoped would be the back of the studio—and an exit.

Blood from her ear dripped onto her neck. She wiped it away again. Shouting came from a distance. Below her, Kim heard scrambling, hissing directions. A bullet pierced her sleeve. She gasped, dropped back against the support wall. Lucky shot or could they see her?

She melted closer into the shadows, imagining herself to *be* a shadow, and waited. There was a sense of movement, but no more bullets. Suddenly, she realized she could see slightly through the hole the bullet had left. A sign on the wall, dimly lit. She moved her head slightly, brought it into focus—a tiny figure of a woman. The sign was for the restrooms.

Which meant she wasn't at all where she thought. Breathing slowly, deeply, to keep herself calm, she waited until she saw the men moving along below her, then began to ease along the wall. If she judged correctly, she could go into the area above the ceiling of the waiting room, then get out through the main doors instead of the back. It didn't make any difference as long as she could get out.

From somewhere, she could hear a television playing. Absurdly, it was a television commercial for cleaning products. In her mind's eye, she saw the dancing scrub brush transforming a dirty bathroom into a clean one. Too bad, she thought, that there were no scrub brushes for the world of wars and politics.

An unexpected and piercing pain caught her right through the middle of the chest. A flash of her brother, grinning.

With a jerk of her head, she shook the picture away. Later. Later she could do whatever screaming she'd like to be doing now. Right now, she had to get the hell out of this television station.

Feeling her way along the wall, she came to another break and eased herself upward to look over the edge again. It was very dark, which meant it was another room with acoustic tiles. How far down from the top of the concrete divider to the ceiling tiles on the other side? She'd have to land carefully or risk putting a foot through the soft material.

She pulled herself up and over the wall, putting all her weight on her arms, then lowering herself slowly, slowly until she felt the tiles against her toe. Hushed voices came up through the acoustic ceiling she stood over. She took a slow, quieting breath.

A flash of light blasted into her eye and she jerked her head in alarm. It was coming from a few feet to her left, a triangular break in the corner of a tile. Bracing herself on the girder, she eased herself down and stretched her body along the ceiling, careful to distribute her weight so an elbow or knee didn't break through. She peered through the triangular break.

Directly below her were three men, one dark and

bearded, with a checkered scarf around his neck and head. He carried an automatic rifle. Another man, older and more routinely dressed in an ordinary shirt and pair of gray slacks, stood to his left. Both of them faced John, the station manager, in his pastel orange shirt. He spoke in Arabic to the other two. It was he who'd been mangling the language.

"Did you find her?" he asked.

"No."

"Keep someone at the doors. She has to come out sometime."

One man headed to the back of the station.

Kim took a breath and quietly let it out.

"We've had an affirmation that Mustafa and Nuri are in place on the way to the airport," John said.

"Very good."

Kim wondered how far it was to the door. If she dropped silently out of the ceiling right by the door, she might be able to make a break for it. Thick sweat pooled over her forehead and dripped into her eye. She blinked hard and rubbed it away with the sleeve of her jacket.

John and the older man moved toward the doors that lead to the studio. The other one, the one who carried the gun, stayed behind, his body posture proclaiming loudly that he was a soldier, used to being a guard.

Perfect.

In the darkness above him, Kim counted to three

hundred to allow the other men a chance to clear out completely. Then, noiselessly, she eased the tile out of its mooring, praying he wouldn't suddenly feel a gust of wind or hear something to tip him off to look up.

He appeared to notice no difference. Kim pulled her body tight into a crouch. It would need exactly the right timing to take him down and avoid getting shot. She waited until he was directly below her. With a cry, she launched herself into the air and catapulted onto his shoulders, knocking the rifle out of his hands.

He fell. The gun flew toward a bank of easy chairs. Kim felt him rearing, grabbing for her legs. She gripped his back ribs with her knees and jabbed the point of her elbow into the long muscle at the base of his skull. Her aim was true: he cried out and collapsed.

A quick search produced a pistol tucked into the small of his back. Kim took it, checked the safety and tucked it under her own coat.

The fight had taken only seconds, and in spite of her yell, the sound of their struggle, it appeared to have drawn no attention.

She bolted out the front doors.

Chapter 7

Snow had begun to fall more heavily in the time Kim had been in the station. How long had it been? She glanced at her watch, found the face cracked, but the display still appeared to be working. She'd been in the station for less than an hour. Snow was already piling up in corners.

In the distance, she heard sirens begin to wail, and realized they were no doubt headed for the station. In no time, the place would be surrounded. She had to get out of there or face getting stuck in the bureaucracy of police questions. The hostages were in danger, there was no question about that, but there was more danger if she didn't get to the airport.

She dashed through the parking lot, checking for an old-model car that she could hot-wire quickly. In the back row, she found what she sought: a 1971 Buick, an old yacht of a car. The door was locked, but Kim pulled out the pistol and used the butt to break the window. She was in.

Three minutes was her record. It took three and a half to hot-wire this one. The sirens whooped closer, into the neighborhood, but not the parking lot. Kim drove the yacht out onto a dark side street that appeared to loop into a residential neighborhood. The vision in her right eye was smeary, and she rubbed it again, trying to clear the viscous fluid.

Now, how the hell would she get to FBI headquarters?

The first order of business was obviously to get herself out of the general area of the station. The chop-chop-chop of a helicopter broke the night, and a cordon of police cars screamed into the parking lot of the UBC station. Their lights turned the sky the pink and blue of cotton candy. Snow glittered down, magically.

As always, Kim thought, Nature was oblivious to the concerns of humans. On Christmas Eve, when this sparkly little snow would be appropriate, she'd bet money it would be dry and sunny.

Kim glided down the street without her lights until she came to an apartment complex on a hill, just a block from the station. She pulled in and parked facing the station, so she could keep an eye on what was going on while she made her calls. A river of police flowed in and surrounded the station like a moat of red lights.

From her jean-jacket pocket, she took her cell phone. The screen showed a waiting message coded from Scott at his desk; the call that had come in while she'd been up in the ceiling. It had only been ten or fifteen minutes. She hoped he was still there and punched in the numbers.

He answered immediately. "Shepherd."

"Thank God you're still there."

"Where are you, Valenti? Chicago is crawling with terrorists. Have you seen the news from the UBC station?"

"Uh…yeah." She wouldn't bother to explain right now. "Scott, there's trouble and I need your help."

"Got it."

"First, I need you to alert the FBI and Chicago security that there is a bomb in the airport somewhere. It's unclear which candidate is targeted, but it's one or the other. They won't believe you, but at least its worth a try. Ask for Lex Tanner. Tell him I said it."

"All right. What else?"

Snow drifted in through the broken window, piling in little tufts on her thigh. Kim brushed it off and turned the heater on a little higher. "I need directions from the UBC office to the FBI office downtown."

"Holy shit, Kim—"

"No time, Shepherd. Just need the information."

"All right, give me a second." She heard him keyboarding in the background.

Her eyebrow stung suddenly, and she scratched it gingerly. With a scowl, she turned the rearview mirror down to look at herself.

Good grief. Blood was smeared all the way down the side of her face and neck. The ear was a mess. The immediate bleeding appeared to have halted, but it was crusty and black with blood, and it was swelling rather impressively, along with her left eye. The cheekbone was going to be downright ugly. Dirt clung to her hair in wisps, and there were scratches and smears and marks all over her.

It was the ear that hurt. And made her look like a refugee from a boxing match. With the fingers of her free hand, she touched it lightly, and even the slightest pressure hurt like crazy. "Ow," she whispered.

"Here's the directions," Scott said. "You ready?"

"Yes." She absorbed the directions by repeating each one. She thanked him.

"Kim," he said in a serious voice. "Please be careful."

"I will, Scott. I promise." She hung up.

Leaving the engine running, she opened the car door and scooped up a small, thin handful of snow. It melted against her hot face, feeling good. In the back seat was a tumble of odds and ends. Kim grabbed a discarded T-shirt. "Sorry, dude," she said aloud to the owner of the car, and used it to wipe away the blood and snow water. When her face looked relatively clean, she grabbed one more handful and rubbed her neck and face one more time.

"Showtime," she said, and put the car in gear.

It was night and snowing when Kim parked at FBI headquarters in Chicago. Snow came in through the window of the stolen car—a 1971 gold Buick Skylark.

Before she got out, she checked her face in the rearview mirror. If there was blood showing, she would draw attention to herself.

There was a bomb, ticking away at the airport. Somewhere. Due to detonate in exactly—she checked her watch—seventy-nine minutes.

In the mirror, she saw that her lip was swollen. She'd have a black eye tomorrow. A few scrapes, but no damage that would make her stand out too much in a law enforcement agency.

She got out of the car and hid the gun she'd stolen in the small of her back, tucked into the waistband of her jeans. The weight of it was comforting and cold. Her cell phone was in her hand, the cord around her wrist.

Snow fell more heavily now, and she was halffrozen from the drive through the Chicago streets in a broken-down car with a shattered window.

Her torn and battered ear throbbed. Without breaking stride, she scooped a handful of snow from the hood of a nearby car and pressed the icy ball to torn cartilage.

As she approached the front doors of the FBI building, a group of men erupted into the parking lot, rushing toward cars and vans. They shouted directions to one another, pulled on gloves, carted cases and rifles.

All headed, no doubt, for the television station. Kim ducked into the shadow of a truck, watching, her mouth hard. She could tell them that their rush was futile, but they wouldn't listen to her now any more than they had earlier.

No, if she had any chance of success, there was only one man for the job—Lex Tanner. She'd believed in him before this morning.

She spied him toward the back of the group, carrying a metal suitcase. His dark hair was cut very short, the nose surprisingly recognizable from the pictures she'd seen, and he was quite tall. At least six-four. Rangy, lean and muscled, with shoulders big enough to shelter her from the wind.

As he neared her spot, she stepped out of the shadows. "Lex Luthor, I presume?"

He started, narrowing his eyes and sizing her up. Recognition washed over his features. "Valenti?" He looked more alarmed than pleased. "Where the hell have you been? I've been calling all afternoon."

"Long story. Right now, I need you to bring your little bomb kit and come with me to the airport."

"I can't. I'm on my way to UBC. There's a terrorist—"

"Yeah, yeah—" she waved a hand "—never mind. That's not the problem."

"They've stolen a bomb they're threatening to detonate—"

"It's not at the station."

"They've got hostages."

"I know." She took a breath. "Look, I don't have time to explain everything, but the drama at UBC is a smoke screen—the bomb is at the airport."

"It's not there! Don't you get it? We've been over it a hundred and forty-seven times."

She pulled out her gun, using her body to shield it from the sight of the others, and poked the barrel into his ribs. "I didn't want to do it this way, but you won't listen."

"What—?"

She glared at him. "Don't make me hurt you, Luthor. I liked you until today."

"This is crazy." He glanced toward the men entering their trucks.

"Don't even think about it." She jabbed the butt into his ribs, harder. "I am dead serious."

"You're going to fuck up your career doing this."

Kim met his eyes. They were extremely blue. She'd read somewhere that extremely blue or green eyes showed a highly sexual nature.

Furious was more the word at the moment.

Oh, well. "Get in the car, and I'll explain."

"You won't shoot me. I know you won't."

"I won't *kill* you," she said. "But I will hurt you if you don't come with me. Now." She pushed harder.

He resisted. "Explain."

She met his eyes with an icy lift of her own eyebrow. "Walk."

He glanced over his shoulder. No one was looking at them. Kim nudged him. "I tried to go through channels, but none of you has given me the respect I deserve, and because of that, people may die unnecessarily."

"If I go against orders, I'll be fired."

"I'm not talking anymore."

His nostrils flared in fury.

"It's killing you to have to listen to a girl, isn't it?"

"No, I—"

"My mother was a nurse in Vietnam. Did you know that? She was taken hostage once for three days, and it's something that has given her nightmares the rest of her life."

"Why the *hell* would I care, Valenti?"

"Because you can trust that I am very, *very* sincere when I say that I hate the whole hostage game. I would do *anything* to free hostages—but I won't let other people die. Do you understand?"

He narrowed his eyes. Damn.

"Luthor, I've had a very bad night. My ear is killing me. There are a couple of bastards at that television station who may or may not kill hostages, but there are law enforcement officials on scene to deal with them. They also don't have a bomb at the station, and that's what I need you for."

"How is it, *Kim*, that you're so much smarter than the entire federal law enforcement community?"

She blinked. "I don't know, *Lex*. You tell me. Maybe I'm just smart. One thing I know for sure is that I *do* know what I'm talking about because—by the way did I tell you I speak Arabic fluently?—I overheard them talking at the television station. There is a bomb or a suicide bomber headed for the airport or *at* the airport, and people will die if we don't go now. I don't know how to defuse a bomb. You do."

"You finished?"

"Yes."

"Let's go. You can explain the rest in the car."

Chapter 8

Lex started the car and turned on the heat to warm it up, but he didn't immediately put the car in gear. "Before I get my ass fired, how 'bout you tell me everything you know?"

"Fair enough." Kim gave Lex a rundown of the evening, the players, everything she knew. He listened, asking questions for clarification now and then.

Without a word, he then picked up his cell phone and called in the details. "I'm going to check it out," he said into the phone, and put the car into gear.

She'd done something to her ankle—probably sprained it jumping from the ceiling—and sitting down now without any need to focus on driving brought the pain out. To join the ones in her face and ear and shoulder.

Tomorrow would *so* not be any fun.

"There's aspirin in the glove box," Lex said.

"How did you know?"

"You keep groaning."

"No, I don't."

He looked at her.

Kim opened the glove box. "How embarrassing."

"Don't worry about it." He flipped on the radio. "Pretty rough in there tonight, huh?"

"I don't want to talk about it. If any of you had just listened to me, I wouldn't have had to try to figure it out on my own. I could be back at the NSA, drinking coffee, basking in saving the day like Nancy Drew."

He chuckled.

Kim's head jerked up. "It's not funny." She hit his arm hard.

"Ow. Ow!" He grabbed her hand when she did it again. "Ow! Quit it. That hurts!"

"It's supposed to."

"You don't hit like a girl at all."

"No kidding. I have four brothers." She blinked at the snow outside the windows. "Three," she amended. "They showed no mercy, trust me."

He put a small red light on top of his car and headed up the freeway. "How much time do we have?"

She looked at the digital display. "About thirty-four minutes."

He raised his brows. "Cutting it a bit close, aren't you?"

"Go to hell, Luthor."

He winked. "Just kidding. I'll get us there."

Traffic was light because of the late hour, but the weather slowed it down. Kim saw a car that had slid into a median. "Must be getting pretty slick."

"Yeah, but I've been driving here since I was twenty. This ain't nothing. Trust me."

And it did seem as if he knew what he was doing, smoothly swooping down the dark, snowy highway, his big hands confident on the wheel. He smelled like cedar, she noticed, and she liked his profile. It was hawkish without too much exaggeration.

"What happened to the fourth brother?" he asked.

"That's pretty straightforward," she returned. "Some might even say rude."

He didn't apologize. "I don't see the point of beating around the bush. You lost a brother. I asked what happened. It's the normal response."

"Yeah, I guess." She blinked. "He would have said, 'Get over yourself.'"

Lex grinned. "My kind of guy."

"He was a soldier in Iraq. He was taken hostage by some rebels and they beheaded him, then gleefully sent the pictures home."

He made a noise of sympathy and horror. "Brutal."

"Yeah. Well, that's war for you."

"I'm sorry. Was he older, younger?"

"One year older. He was a good soldier. He really loved it."

"How'd your mother feel about that?"

"She nearly killed him when he enlisted."

"I can imagine. A combat nurse sees a lot of damage."

Kim nodded.

He switched lanes, glanced at the clock, shifted. "We'll be there in about five minutes."

"Good." The adrenaline of the evening was draining away, leaving her achy, exhausted and ready for a stiff vodka and a hot bath. Taking in a deep breath, she focused away from her body. Lex was handy, something to focus on.

Or so she told herself. It wasn't as if it was a hardship. There was drama in his face. His right eyebrow was sharply arched, very dark. His eyes were a little larger than normal, much bluer. His nose was aggressive, his mouth wide, the lips sensual, with the upper just a little bigger than the lower. A sign of generosity in love.

He glanced at her. "You all right?"

"Fine."

"I have three sisters," he said. "All older."

"Oh, God. I should have known. You were spoiled rotten, too, weren't you?"

"You better believe it. Damn!" He downshifted

suddenly, and Kim's attention jolted forward. There were lines of red brake lights ahead, coming too fast through the swirling snow.

Lex downshifted, braked lightly, glided to a stop. "No way," he muttered. "Hold on. We've got to go around."

He nosed across the lanes, the flashing light giving them access to small breaks in the sea of vehicles. He edged through, all the way across six lanes, then onto the shoulder, which was largely clear.

Kim looked for the accident, and there it was, of course: a tangle of cars, none looking seriously damaged, blocking every single lane. Drivers were out of their cars, some shouting at each other, gesturing, some on cell phones.

"Gonna be some missed flights tonight," Lex said.

"I'm surprised how much traffic there is so late," Kim replied. The anxiety in her chest trebled.

"It's a busy airport."

"Let's just get there."

The clock on the dashboard said 11:32 when Lex slid into the departure area and left the car. "C'mon."

Kim dashed out behind him, wincing at the bright lights inside after so long an evening. They hurried toward the security lines, where a short line of people waited to go through the X-ray machines. A woman in a wheelchair blocked their way through a narrow area, and they paused, waiting for her to get through.

Lex glanced at Kim. "You look like hell, Valenti. That's gonna be a shiner and a half tomorrow."

"Won't matter if we don't find the—uh—package, will it?"

The number of milling human beings was not huge, not as it would have been at noon or at 5 p.m. It was enough, though. More than enough for a cataclysm. The guard, a young woman with a long yellow braid, waved the wheelchair woman through. Kim flashed on her ordeal at the Baltimore airport earlier today.

Only today?

It seemed years ago.

Lex obviously knew his way around. He lifted his hand at the girl with the braid. She didn't flirt, as Kim might have suspected. Her eyes were trained on a television playing by a bank of telephones and vending machines. The screen showed an aerial shot of the UBC station, surrounded by police cars.

Kim's ear throbbed. She put a hand up to cover it protectively.

Lex waved her through ahead of him, leading her down a hallway. "You really do look terrible," he said. "No offense."

"I assure you that however terrible the appearance, the reality is quite a lot worse."

He quirked his lips, holding open a door for her to go through ahead of him. "I've got a claw-footed bathtub at my place. You could soak up to your ears."

She winced. "Don't say ear."

"What?"

"Never mind." She shook hair out of her eyes. "Where's Monihan landing? Do we know that?"

"Concourse E. There's a special area for VIP landings like this."

"Where're we headed, then?"

"Cameras. We can get a look at the airport as a whole, see if we can get a handle on who or what we might need to explore by looking at the waiting areas."

"Hmm. Very smart."

He grinned. The teeth were large and white. A dimple flashed in his left cheek.

Wretched thing. "I've done this once or twice," he said.

She glanced at her watch—11:41.

"Chill, sweetheart. Getting tense gets you nothin' but jittery." He tapped his temple with one finger. "Cool and sweet leaves the brain intact."

"Whatever."

Lex knocked and was given access to a large room behind a heavy steel door. Banks of television screens showed dozens of views of the airport—security lines at the mouth of each concourse, gate areas, hallways, restaurants and bars, bookstores and shops. Kim stared at the vastness of them, the numbers of places to look, the dizzying number of people. Even a glance at each one would take way too long.

"Now what?"

"Now, darlin'," he said, "you access that brain of yours and see if you can see anybody who might fit a pattern. Don't get too caught up in what you think you know. Let your gut talk to you."

"Gotta narrow it down," she said, blinking her grainy eyes. "Anybody have any Visine or anything?"

A guy in a security uniform grabbed a bottle from his desk. He tossed it at her. Kim dropped her head back and let the drops cool and soothe her overheated eyes.

Lex swore.

Kim glared at him, blinking. "What?"

But he wasn't looking at the screens. With one long-fingered hand, he reached out and lifted up the hair that covered the side of her face. He whistled. "They'll call you Cauliflower Kim after this," he said with a grin. "You're tough, ain't ya?"

She tilted her head away, and he dropped her hair. She looked back to the screens. "Couple questions. Is the president gone?"

"No. Air Force One is on the ground," said a man with wild grizzled eyebrows and a serious paunch. "Not here, though. He's flying out of a private airfield twenty miles away. Standard procedure."

"Good. How about Monihan?"

"He'll dock here." The man pointed to the end of the screens, then waved a finger around to the gates—most of them empty—that were close by. "These gates are pretty close. He'll come in on the lower level. This is upstairs."

Lex frowned.

Kim said, "I think we're probably looking for a man and a woman, or maybe two women."

"That narrows it down."

She peered at one gate after another. Anxiety ratcheted up in her gut, burning through her esophagus.

Or maybe that was hunger. She rubbed her diaphragm. "Why can't we just clear the airport?"

"Presidential edict," the security boss said. "After what happened in Spain, we're trying not to overreact to terrorist demands. Ever."

"I hardly think closing the airport is overreacting. Not when there's strong evidence that a suicide bomber could be ready to kill hundreds of people." She turned to meet his eye. "Is it?"

He lifted a shoulder. "It's not my call, unfortunately."

One of the other security guards cleared his throat. "All right, so if they got a bomb through security, how could they do it? We're x-raying, searching, swabbing, everything. How could they?"

"I don't know that answer," Kim said.

"Where there's a will, there's a way," Lex said. Again she noticed the timbre of his voice. Rich. He put his hands on his hips as he examined the screens. "The trick is just to work around the paradigms."

"What's that mean?" the kid asked, offended. "What else can we do?"

"Nothing," Lex said. "Don't be offended. It's just a way of looking at reality."

Kim peered at one screen after another, seeing nothing at all amiss. A man in a shiny, waterlike robe and a binding around his head caught her eye. He strode with an arrogant lilt toward one end of the concourse. A small girl danced along beside him, and a woman with a child on either side was just behind. Her gut said, *no.*

And it made her feel faintly ill to be profiling like that, anyway, looking for Middle Eastern sorts of faces—a vast region and a vast number of people and countries. Only a handful had caused trouble for the United States.

Behind her, Lex said, "A paradigm is just a way to think about things. Like before 9/11, nobody questioned the wisdom of agreeing to the demands of a hijacker. It was the smart thing to do, right?"

"Sure," said the kid.

"The reason those hijackers could overtake the planes was because they worked with that paradigm. Now, the paradigm has shifted—you never give in to a hijacker—and because of that, nobody can hijack a plane. The passengers won't allow it."

Kim felt an inkling itch through the back of her brain. "So, to get a bomb through security, somebody just has to think outside the box."

"Exactly."

She turned back to the screens. "I think we might be looking for a woman," she said, and quoted the phrase they'd found repeatedly in the e-mails, *"'Good women are obedient. They guard their unseen parts because Allah has guarded them. Surah 4:34.'"*

"What does that mean?"

"It was in the e-mails we decoded. It's from the Koran." She frowned. "Something happened earlier today that made me feel there was some intelligence about women that might not have been passed on." She lifted an eyebrow. "By accident, I'm sure. We know all information is equally available to all agencies."

"Mmm. All right, then." Lex stood beside her. "Let's look for women in that general area who might be suspicious in some way."

They all peered at the screens. There were cameras showing various angles of the concourse, in grainy black-and-white. The women Kim spotted all looked perfectly ordinary—businesswomen in slacks and button-up blouses; mothers in stretch jeans; students showing three inches of skin between shirt and pants. She saw a gathering of Muslim women, plump and shrouded, but they had enough babies and children between them that she doubted seriously they were hiding anything. So far, mothers had not been big suicide bombers.

Nothing looked out of place. Kim rubbed her eyes again, exhaustion burning down her spine. She looked for women who moved oddly, not like a woman.

And suddenly, she said, "Look." She stabbed a finger to a woman in a straight black skirt and loose print blouse with long sleeves. Her head was covered by a traditional scarf. On her feet were plain Keds.

All perfectly normal, except the fact that she carried a leather case. Kim said, "What's she doing with a laptop?"

"Dammit," Lex said. "I just figured out a possibility. C'mon."

Kim rushed after him. They ran, Lex carting his heavy case, Kim behind him nonetheless. The ankle hurt, but she was trained to ignore pain. It was a long run, through the main sections of the airport, then into security at the concourse. The guards waved them through.

On the concourse itself, they slowed to a normal walk, to avoid alerting the possible terrorists, but Kim felt sweat trickling down her back.

"I thought laptops were x-rayed," she said.

"They are. It won't be the laptop itself that's the bomb—it'll be used as a power source. A spark of electricity will set it off. You can use almost anything—a phone, a razor, but the more current, of course, the better the spark."

Kim felt queasy. How did people blow themselves up? Actually *do* it? "That still doesn't answer the question of how they got the bomb through security."

"I don't know. We'll have to use our instincts."

The gate they'd spotted on the monitors was a long way down the concourse, close to the outskirts where the private jets landed. But this plane was packed, headed for Los Angeles, and the area was crowded. Kim watched a slim blond mother chase her cherubic toddler around a suitcase. A young man walked slowly beside his grandmother, who hung on to his arm for support.

Kim had a sudden flash of body parts flying. "Let's find this bastard," she said.

"There she is," Lex said. "By the window."

Kim slowed. "I see her."

"Let's go easy. She's probably not alone."

She made a sweeping examination of the area. A lot of the usual suspects. Businessmen in khaki pants and polo shirts. Families headed for Disneyland. California types in pastel. She thought about John at the UBC television station, and looked carefully at the men of his ilk. But he'd looked perfectly ordinary. Nothing written across his forehead that said, "I'm a traitor who colludes with terrorists."

If only it were that easy.

The woman behind the desk picked up the microphone, and in a too-loud address over the PA system, she announced, "Good evening, ladies and gentlemen. Welcome to our service to Los Angeles tonight. We are about to start preboarding, so…"

People shifted, started gathering their belongings, and the hair on the back of Kim's neck stood up straight. This would be the time to do it. This plane boarding; Monihan's plane coming in. Her watch said 11:53.

"We don't want her to plug that laptop in," Lex said. His eye was on the woman, sitting with the computer in her lap. For some reason, Kim noticed how long and graceful her fingers were, wrapping around the edge of the black plastic. Beautifully shaped oval nails, smooth pale skin.

"Let's go. We aren't going to know who her backup is until we act anyway."

The woman shifted her position as they approached, her attention fixed intently upon something in her hands. The door to one hallway was to the left, the milling passengers spread out all around them. She wiped her brow with a sleeve, and the truth slammed Kim.

"That's not a woman."

"Damn. C'mon."

Kim started to run, but in that instant, she caught sight of two other men, headed for them. She tried to reach the one with the laptop, but everything happened at once.

A burly, mustachioed man barreled into her, his arm capturing her arms close to her body so she could not swing. The unmistakable nose of a gun jammed into her ribs. She froze.

Lex bellowed, "Clear the area!"

The area exploded. People started screaming, running, banging into each other. Suitcases fell over. The PA system announced a different flight.

Using the momentary distraction, Kim dropped her body straight down and whirled in a circle, making herself a snake who slid out of her assailant's grip. She was ready for his gun, grabbing his wrist as she sank, and managed to shove it away from her body just as he fired. The bullet skidded over the skin of her side in a burning hot line, and she heard someone grunt behind her.

The screaming of terrified passengers, businessmen and families trebled. A man tripped on a suitcase right in front of her and slammed down, face-first. His glasses shattered, but Kim had no time to help him.

Struggling with the man who was so much stronger than she, she had to be fast. She slammed her captor's hand against a nearby chair. The gun skittered away on the waxed floor beneath a bank of chairs. The terrorist grabbed her, his fingers digging into her neck, and she slammed her head back as hard as she could, connecting with something hard— chin or teeth—then used her elbow to knock the wind out of his lungs.

He fell backward with a grunt. Kim yanked herself free, and slammed the butt of her own gun against the back of his head. He slumped into unconsciousness.

Breathing hard, she looked around for the "woman" with the laptop. Nowhere to be seen. "Damn!"

Lex had subdued his captor and breathing heavily, looked toward Kim "Where did the woman go?" she cried.

He pointed. "Ladies' room." He wiped a hand over his face and winced. His right hand was bloody and he looked at it with anger. "Goddammit," he growled.

It was only then that Kim saw the injury, a bullet hole through the lower section of his palm. She yanked off her coat and ran toward him. "Here. Wrap it up."

"There's no time!" He shoved her toward the ladies' room. "You're going to have to dismantle the bomb. Let's go."

"Right."

There were several women cowering inside the restroom, but Kim didn t immediately see the one she was looking for. Pressing her finger to her lips for silence, she jerked her thumb over her shoulder to indicate they should all get out quietly. With whispers and murmurs and more commotion than Kim would have liked, they did so. She ducked to see under the stalls. In the back, she spied the Keds she was looking for.

Glancing back at Lex, who moved behind her with his hand—dripping blood—held above his head, she pointed to the stall. He nodded.

With a smooth movement, Kim dived under the metal wall, and grabbed the terrorist above the ankle. It was surprisingly thin.

He yelped, and tried to yank away. Kim held tight. A spate of Arabic poured from his mouth, babbling and incoherent. Kim slid all the way into the stall, and using her body to trap him between the wall and her arm, she cried, "I've got him!" and unlocked the stall door for Lex.

"Haul him out here."

Kim shifted her weight, flung the boy toward the floor. She landed on top of him, trapping his arms beneath her wrists. Lex opened his silver case. Blood dripped off his elbow to splash to the floor.

"Where is the bomb?" Kim asked in Arabic. He was much younger than she first thought—a boy of perhaps seventeen, and he was weeping, tears pouring down his smooth brown cheeks. Was he afraid? Or was it shame? Shame at being dressed as a woman, apprehended in a women's toilet?

Cruel to give a boy such an assignment, Kim thought.

A cruelty that paled in comparison to making him blow himself up, she supposed, and shoved her arm against his throat hard. "Where is the bomb?" she cried.

He jerked his chin downward. "Breasts," he said in English.

Kim scrambled backward, shoved open the blouse he wore to expose the bra beneath. It was an underwire model, heavily stuffed with a thick, breast-shaped plastic. The white nylon fabric of the bra against the boy's smooth young skin gave her a pain.

What kind of world killed off its young like this, as soldiers and martyrs?

"What do I do?" she asked Lex. "Take it off of him?"

"Please," said the youth in Arabic. "I do not want to die."

For a minute, Kim's gaze flew to his face. His plea moved her.

Lex said behind her, "He's lying."

She looked over her shoulder. "What?"

"It's a time pencil. He's buying time."

The boy spit at her, and Kim had to scramble to avoid losing hold of him. At the idea that the bomb could explode at any second, she felt suddenly, faintly ill, and had to physically fight the urge to leap away from him. A shudder violently shook her spine. "What do we do?"

"See where the bra comes together? Insert this pin there, very slowly."

Kim held the boy with her knees. He jerked, and she slammed his arms down hard. In Arabic, she said, "If you move, and I live through you blowing us up, I'll tell everyone you peed your pants you were so scared."

He spit again. Instinctively, she hit him, and he slumped backward, at least dazed, if not unconscious.

"Take the little tube there, and ease it out," Lex said.

Very gently, Kim gripped what looked like an eyebrow pencil and eased it out of its spot. On the end was a little cap. "This?"

"Yeah. Easy." Lex leaned in. "Hold your boy."

Kim braced herself more firmly against the kid, and Lex very gently touched the pencil cap. He took a breath, moved it ever so slightly, then let go of his breath. "That was the moment we could have blown."

"Thanks for telling me."

"Anytime. Now," he said in that smooth, low voice. "You gently wiggle the cap free, and there'll be a wire underneath, which we're going to cut."

"All right. But our explosion moment is passed?"

"Not exactly."

"Oh." Kim eased the cap upward, spied the wires beneath. "Now what?"

Lex braced the cap in his fingers and lifted his chin to the bomb kit. "Cut it."

"Do I die here?" she asked, taking the scissors from the kit.

"Not if you do it right." His eyes were a vivid blue,

and twinkling enough that she thought he might be teasing her. "That's what I'm here for, remember?"

"Right." Kim squeezed her eyes shut, opened them, cut the wire, and whooped, pulling it free from the bomb.

Kim slumped in relief, and wiped sweat from her upper lip. "How did he get that through security?"

"Paradigms," Lex said simply. "What guard is going to pat down actual breasts? And metal detectors react to bras all the time. The underwires and hooks and clips. It's understood. We're not prepared—who would be?—for people who blow themselves up."

His face was as white as the porcelain surrounding them. Blood had pooled beneath his elbow in a sticky, spreading mass. "That's bad." She stood up and yanked the belt out of her jeans, then knelt and tied it around his arm. "We need to get you to the hospital."

"I'll be fine in an hour or two." He held out his good hand. "Where the hell is everybody, anyway?" He coughed. "Let me use your phone to call security."

She pulled it out of her pocket, and handed it over to him. The Arab boy was breathing harshly, but he'd survive. Lex took the phone and punched in some numbers, and Kim stood up to get a thick pile of paper towels from the dispenser on the wall. She carried them back to where Lex slumped against the wall, and dropped some on the ground to absorb the blood there, and then sandwiched the gory hand between two layers of towels and pressed hard from both sides.

"All clear," Lex said into the phone, and gave directions to their location. "We need medical assistance. I've been shot—not seriously, but it hurts like hell."

His eyes were on Kim's face. They were as blue as a teacup her mother had once brought home from a fair. She looked away, down to the hand pressed between her palms.

"Hey," he said.

Kim raised her face. "Hey, yourself."

"Good work."

"You, too."

It was impulsive and probably foolish, but she did it anyway, gripped his hand between hers. Kissed him. And didn't pull away immediately. His free hand came up behind her head and caught her, and his lips opened with a little growl, inviting her in. She tasted sweat—hers or his, she wasn't sure—and a faint hint of cloves, which must be him. Close up, she caught a hint of Indian spice. "Curry?" she said, pulling back.

"It's in the leather. I practically live in an Indian restaurant nearby my apartment." He tugged her down to him again.

His lips were as richly generous as they looked.

His tongue swirled against hers, sending a jolt of thick excitement down her spine. Abruptly, she pulled back. "Bad idea."

He looked at her. "Is it?"

"We're just reacting to the danger."

"Maybe." His voice was gravelly, that Southern drawl like honey on her neck. "Maybe we're just reacting to each other."

"It's been a long night," Kim said, suddenly aware of her headache. She sat down on the floor with a thump and pressed her palms to her temples. "A long damned day."

"You need to let them look at you at the hospital, too," he said. "We'll ride together."

Kim realized it was over, finally. "God, I'm tired."

"Good job, kiddo," he said. "You saved the world tonight."

"Maybe not the *world*."

"A big piece of mine."

Kim took a breath, but at that moment, security swarmed in and there wasn't a chance to say any more.

Chapter 9

At the hospital emergency room, they were separated. Lex was wheeled into one examining room. Kim went to one in another direction. Sitting in the sterile white room, with fluorescent light turning the air a faint green, she discovered she was a long way beyond exhaustion.

All at once, the day caught up with her, and she fell backward on the table like a drunk who'd had one too many. Her head spun. Her ear throbbed, her ankle ached, her face felt as if it had been a punching bag—which she supposed it had been. Even her teeth ached.

She had awakened—she glanced with effort toward a clock on the wall, since it was too much effort to raise her wrist—nineteen hours ago. Since then, she'd gone to the office as usual. Flown to Chicago. Fought off a creepy man with no expression who'd very nearly killed her, jumped a terrorist, stolen a car, kidnapped an FBI agent and defused a bomb.

Her stomach felt positively hollow. She was *hungry*. Starving. Her stomach was making little hollow noises like a tired puppy. With effort she lifted a hand and put it over the grumbling.

She must have drifted off, her feet swinging free at the end of the table, because the next thing she knew, a warm female voice was saying, "Ms Valenti, can you tell me where you're hurting?"

"What?" She opened both eyes, but it was too bright, so she closed one. "Ear," she said, and added thickly, "Starving."

The woman, a plump blonde with exotic blue eyes, chuckled. "Let's see," she said with a frown, and searched her pockets, coming up with a banana and a chocolate bar. "Want them?"

"Banana," Kim said, just as her stomach growled again.

The woman laughed again. Such a lilting, pleasant sound. "Why don't you have both? I might want to give you some painkillers." She lifted Kim's hair to look at her ear. "Ooh, that hurts a lot, I betcha. You need some stitches, I suspect. Where else?"

One by one, Kim let the doctor check out her injuries, large and small. Black eye, torn ear, bruised face, cut lip, burn where the bullet had buzzed by her skin, sprained ankle. She devoured the banana, then the chocolate bar, and happily accepted a painkiller with a glass of water. Somebody could get her to the hotel and she could pour herself into bed.

With a Do Not Disturb sign on the door.

As she cleaned up Kim's ear, the doctor said, "You're all over the news, you know—big heroes, the pair of you."

"It was him, not me."

"Oh, no, you don't. Wait till you see the news."

Kim remembered the situation at the television station. "Did they get the hostages out?"

"Yeah. No worries. A SWAT team took the station about an hour and a half ago. Two of the terrorists managed to escape, but none of the hostages were hurt."

"That's good." She thought about asking for the details of which ones had escaped and decided to let it go for tonight. Enough already.

"Hang on, this will pinch a little." A needle the size of the Eiffel Tower arrived at the edge of Kim's peripheral vision and she closed her eyes tight. The pinch was not pleasant, but immediately afterward, a blessed numbness spread through the ear.

Kim let go of a breath. "Oh, that's good. It was really hurting!"

"It's pretty battered." The distant sound of scissors, and Kim assumed the doctor was starting the stitches. "Wait'll you see the video they're running of you."

"Me?" Kim said. "Where did they get video of me?"

"It's from the television station. You dropped out of a ceiling and knocked out a terrorist with a gun, just like a movie or something."

"Oh. That."

The doctor laughed. "That! It's pretty exciting stuff. You were brave."

"I'm very well trained."

"So what!" The doctor leaned her face around to look Kim in the eye. "I saw what you did. It was tough."

"Thanks."

Lex appeared in the threshold. His hand was bandaged. "You're a hero," he said.

"That's what I was just telling her," said the doctor.

"Yeah, yeah. You're the hero, Mr. Luthor."

"As in Martin Luther?" the doctor asked, peering over her half glasses.

"No, that would be Lex Luthor, the archvillain in *Superman*," Kim said.

The doctor laughed appreciatively, but went back to stitching up Kim's ear. Kim looked at Lex. He looked pale and drawn, but maybe he always looked like that—how would she know?

"You're all set," the doctor said, gathering up her tools and stripping off her gloves. "Keep it clean and dry and go see your doctor back home in five to seven days."

"Thanks." Kim slid off the table. Looked at Lex. "Is someone going to take me to the hotel now?"

"Well—"

"What does that mean?"

He drew her out into the hallway. His bandaged hand was caught in a sling, making it look as if he were saying the Pledge of Allegiance. "There are hordes of reporters waiting for you there."

"I don't care. I'll just blow them off and go to my room."

"It's not that. I don't think you'll be safe there."

"Safe from whom?"

His lips quirked upward. "La-ti-ta. From terrorists, sweetheart."

"Oh." She blinked. "Can't we find me a hotel somewhere else?"

"We could. But it's easier to guard my place, and I've got a spare bedroom."

"No," she said. Overwhelmed with weariness, she said, "I just can't stand that weirdness. I'm sorry."

"Weirdness?"

"Yeah." They were standing in a waiting area. Gray-and-white tiles ran in a long pattern beneath their feet. She stuck the envelope with her pills in her jeans pocket. "There's this—tension—between us.

And I like it, don't get me wrong, but I'm just too wiped—"

"Hey." He caught her jaw in two fingers of his good hand. "None of that. Swear."

"It's not just you, you know."

A faint smile made crow's-feet show around his eyes. "You mean you might sneak into my bed in the middle of the night and ravish me?"

His eyes were practically neon. She thought again of that study that said intensely colored eyes meant high sex drive. The thought sent pings of wishfulness through her belly. "Maybe."

He grinned more broadly, dropped his hand. "I'd probably live through it."

Tension rose in her neck, and she wanted to slap someone. Which would be worse? Media blitz with possible terrorists lurking to blow her away in her room, or sleeping at the apartment of a man she liked? "Oh, never mind," she said irritably. "Let's just go."

He gestured with an open palm. Bowed slightly. "To my castle, then, my lady."

Kim rolled her eyes. "What planet are you from, Luthor?"

He chuckled. "There's a car waiting for us." He led the way toward the entrance. Before they arrived, however, it was plain the media interest was not only grouped at her hotel. A swarm of camera-toting reporters was clustered around the hospital entrance. Lights shone from trucks.

"I'm *so* not in the mood," Kim growled.

"Just give 'em that look, honeypie, and you'll be safe."

She glared up at him. "Isn't it 'sugarpie'?"

"Either one'll do." He pushed the doors open and the reporters swarmed, buzzing out questions, shoving microphones forward, running cameras. Kim put up her hand against the glare of one bright light, and grimaced at the cameraman who held it.

The questions rained down:

"Do you think there are more terrorist attacks planned for Chicago?"

"Ms. Valenti, tell us how you learned to fight like a commando!"

"Tell us about the Athena Academy."

"Hey, Tanner, is it serious?"

"Is there a connection between tonight's actions and the unrest in Berzhaan?"

At this last question, Kim stopped dead on the sidewalk. "Uh, yeah." She tapped her forehead in frustration. "You might have picked that up since they *told* us that at the television station!"

"Don't worry about them," Lex said, his good hand at the small of her back.

She ducked into the back seat of an unmarked sedan that screamed GOVERNMENT CAR in every detail: the navy blue color, the crisp new smell inside, a blandness so overt as to be suspicious.

It was warm and dry. That was what mattered.

The young marine driving turned around to make sure they were settled. "Anything I can get you two before we head out?"

"Can I get my bag from the hotel?"

"We already took care of that for you, ma'am. It might not get to Mr. Tanner's place till morning, but you'll have your things.'

"I really wanted my toothbrush."

"Don't worry," Lex said, "I've got spares."

Dryly, she said, "Of course you do."

As the car pulled away from the hospital and the crowd of reporters, both Lex and Kim fell back against the seat, heads back. Kim closed her eyes. "Even my eyelashes hurt," she said.

"I bet." He touched her hand, and it wasn't threatening. It was…nice. She didn't move hers away. "I bet you're starving, too, aren't you?"

"The doctor gave me a banana." She paused, dug up the rest of the words from some deep well. "Chocolate bar, too."

"Gosh, all of that?" His thumb moved on her inner palm, slow and comforting.

His hand was large and competent, not clammy. Kim let her index finger explore the hair on his wrist. "Yeah, it wasn't really enough," she admitted. "I could eat a cow."

"I probably have some steaks in the freezer. Wouldn't take long to thaw them out."

Kim groaned. "Oh, God, Luthor! Who could cook

at a time like this? We're both exhausted. Fast food will do. There's a McD's right there, have the guy stop."

"Fast food, Valenti?" He gave her a mocking shake of the head. "Forget it. I don't put that stuff in my body."

She raised an eyebrow. "What, you eat organically or something?"

He nodded. "Since 2000."

"Does that mean you chant and do yoga and wear hemp underwear?"

His chuckle was ragged. Loose and sexy. His thumb moved over her palm. "You want to see my underwear?"

"Not today." Her stomach growled. "Okay, Mr. Perfect World, make the man stop for me so I can get a chemical burger for my poor belly."

"We're almost at my apartment. Trust me—I have much better food there." His fingers looped through hers. "Fast food is one of my geeky issues, all right? We're all allowed."

Kim turned her head to look at him in disbelief. Yep. Same guy. Same chiseled profile. Strong jaw. Gorgeous cheekbones. He had a bullet wound in his hand and had saved the airport from a terrorist bomb. "Fast food," she echoed. "You don't eat fast food."

He took a breath, turned his head to look back at her. Both of them sprawled with their heads against the seat, and when he looked at her, his face really was very close. Light flashed over the bridge of his nose, flickered over his irises, shadowed now with the minklike eyelashes. "My mother is an activist. She pounded it into my head."

"Ah. Your mother did it." She rolled her eyes. "That makes it all better."

"Watch it, Valenti."

"Or what?" Her nostrils quivered with suppressed laughter. "You'll slap me?"

His mouth was only inches from her own. She felt his breath brush her lips when he said, "I'll kiss you again."

"I kissed you, remember?"

He didn't move anything except his index finger, which swirled around and around the heart of her palm. A light swirling movement that might have been annoying if it hadn't been so arousing. "So you did," he agreed.

She turned her head away.

The apartment was in a prewar-era building, six brick stories. Kim was dismayed, but let go of a sigh of relief when she saw the elevators.

"What's that about?" Lex asked.

"My ankle is honestly killing me. I didn't want to climb any stairs."

It was a beautiful building, garnished with art deco touches throughout—fan-shaped light covers in the hallways, ornate giltwork on the elevator sculpted into women and serpents. "Pretty tony stuff for an FBI agent," she said, following him into the box. The doors slid shut.

"It belonged to my grandmother," Lex said. "She knew I loved the place."

"Nice." She was trying to keep her weary brain out of the gutter, trying not to like everything about him so damned much. His hands, lean and long, looked capable and strong. Prickles of gold and reddish hair bristled on his chin, and she thought she'd like to watch him shave. It was even more intriguing that some of the details of his life didn't sync with the profile of a rough-and-ready bomb expert.

Like the apartment itself. It smelled cool and, faintly, of the curry he'd said he loved. In her experience, men were at best minimalists when it came to decorating. It was lucky when there weren't dirty socks piled up in armchairs and six years of bacterial growth in the toilets.

This was not minimalist at all. There were overstuffed armchairs with textured upholstery rivets in swirls around the arms, and big ottomans, and a couch that looked as if it could comfortably seat twelve, piled high with pillows in green and gold. It had obviously been furnished by a woman, but there were manly touches, too, things Lex must have added—large vintage travel photos of cars, boats, planes. A newspaper framed with headlines about D-day. "God, that's a beauty," she said, leaning forward to look at it.

"Yeah, I found it at a Goodwill. Ain't that something? C'mon in the kitchen, sweetheart. I'll get you a beer."

"Oh, yeah. I would sell my *soul* for a beer," she breathed.

"Not necessary. I'll just give you one." He tossed his keys on the counter of the kitchen, flicked on the overhead light. "Dark okay?"

"I don't care."

He pulled out a couple of brown bottles and opened them with a church key. Kim looked around. The floors were made of very tiny tiles, a little old and discolored in places, but mostly very well kept. "This is fantastic."

"Thanks." He lifted his bottle with his left hand and took a long, serious swallow. Kim remembered he'd had a hell of a day, too. It showed in the hollows beneath his eyes. "She did a lot of work before she died, but I've done a lot, too. Some of the stuff is remodeled back to the original styles, but some of it is the real thing. Notice the bathroom, will you? I'm too beat to give you the grand tour tonight."

"I'm too tired to appreciate it."

He stood up. "Food, though. We need food."

"Lex, really, it doesn't matter."

"Don't be ridiculous. I'm not going to let you go to bed without supper." He stuck his head in the fridge. "Ah, here we go." He slapped a container of cracked olives and a brick of cheese on the counter.

"This'll tide us over while I make an omelet. Faster than steak. How does that sound?"

"You can't cook with that hand."

"Honey, if you weren't here, I'd do it. You may as well let me give you some of it, too. Open the olives. I can't do that part. And you're going to have to slice the cheese."

She whisked the lid off the plastic container. The smell of honest-to-goodness Italian olives made her groan. She put one in her mouth and closed her eyes at the burst of flavor. "Oh, the real thing."

"Yeah, you're an Italian girl, aren't you?" He grinned. "My Nana, she's the one who had this apartment, she was Sicilian. It's her buddy's granddaughter who runs the deli around the corner."

"That's where you got that nose."

"The deli?" He shoved the cheese, a knife and a plastic cutting board toward her.

"Ha. The grandmother." She picked up the knife. "Thin?"

A nod. He took out other things: a carton of organic eggs, goat cheese, tomatoes with green vine still attached. "It's weird that you eat organically, Mr. Luthor. It's just so not in keeping with your tough-guy image."

He quirked a dark brow. "Do you know what they do to chickens?"

She grinned. "I'm not sure whether I should answer yes or no. If I say yes, and I know but still use regular eggs, I'm a bit of a slime, huh?"

"Nah." He put a blue bowl down on the tiny tiles of the counter. "But I'd recommend never mentioning it in front of my mother."

"Oh, shit!" She slapped her forehead. "I need to call my mother."

"It's two in the morning!"

"Three on the East Coast. But if she saw me on television jumping a terrorist, she won't sleep until she hears from me." She pulled out her cell phone and punched in the speed dial #1, and put the phone to her ear.

"Aw, that's cute, Valenti. Momma's #1."

She flipped him off and ducked her head away as her mother said in her ear, "Kim?"

"I'm fine, Mom. Totally fine."

"What were you thinking? You don't have to be a cowboy! You could have been killed."

Kim ran a thumbnail along the seam of her jeans and let her mother say all the things she needed to say, all the stuff that she needed to get out because the worry had made her crazy. When she paused, Kim said, "Are you done?"

"Yes. Thanks." She took a breath. "Who's the good lookin' man you were at the hospital with?"

"How'd you know about that?"

"It was on television. Not ten minutes ago. CNN."

"We were on CNN?" Kim scowled, pointed over Lex's shoulder to the television sitting on a counter in the corner. "There was video at the hospital?"

"I just said that!" A murmur in the background. "Your father says he looks Italian."

"Yeah, well, he's part Sicilian, but don't get your hopes up. These Chicago Sicilians are all connected to the mob, I hear. He'll probably cut off my feet or something." She looked at Lex and pressed her finger to her lips.

He mimed zipping his mouth shut and turned on the television.

"Mom," Kim said, "Kiss Dad for me. I've been up for way, way too long."

"Call when you get home, baby."

"Will do." She flipped the phone closed and set it on the counter. "How much cheese?"

"A couple of ounces. A little extra to nibble."

Kim followed orders, and when he got to the eggs, she held out her hand. "You want me to do it?"

He grinned. "Nope." With a flourish, he took an egg from the carton and cracked it smartly against the edge of a red ceramic bowl, then deftly opened it with one hand.

"Nice." Out of the corner of her eye, she saw a slither of black fur slide around the corner. "Hey! A cat!"

"That's Velvet."

"Very original."

"He came with the apartment."

"Here kitty, kitty, kitty," Kim called softly, holding out her hand. The cat was enormous, all black with yellow eyes, and his body was covered with thick shiny fur. He settled in the doorway and looked at her. "He's a very Egyptian cat, isn't he?"

Lex glanced at the cat. "Huh. So he is. I never thought about it, but you're right—he should be guarding a pyramid."

"Will he mind if I pet him?"

"No," Lex said. "He just likes you to chase him around some."

"Ah. How very like a man." She made quiet, coaxing noises, little girl noises, and approached the cat. He arched his back, trotted away, came back, rubbed her leg. "Hey, guy." He started to purr.

"Don't get any ideas, now," Lex said, stirring eggs vigorously with a fork. "He sleeps with me. Non-negotiable."

Kim laughed. "I had you pegged all wrong. I figured you to be a big-dog, bloody-steak kind of guy."

"Pretty cliché," he said, and added with a wink, "Baby." He jerked his head toward the stove. "I need your help for a sec."

Kim let the cat go and moved to the stove. "What?"

Their bodies were very close. His aggressive, beautiful nose and lush mouth were right in front of her. His right hand was still clasped in the sling close to his chest, but his other hand came up around her neck. "I just wanted to kiss you again." he said.

"Easy," Kim said.

"Right."

The first time, Kim had been buzzing from adrenaline. This time she decided the buzz was from exhaustion. She got lost for a minute, tasting the plumpness of that lower lip, the suggestion of tongue just behind it. She drifted into it, their heads moving, their bodies still.

He lifted his head. "Nice."

"We really shouldn't be messing around like this. We're too tired. The situation is too charged."

He raised his eyebrows, nodded. "You're right," he said, sounding as if he meant the opposite. "Now, would you put that skillet on the stove for me, darlin'?"

"Skillet?" she repeated. "You mean the frying pan?"

"Don't get smart with me."

She moved the pan and stepped back, watching as he poured the eggs into the pan and swirled them around. His elbow and forearm were stringed with muscle, and she liked his competence in the kitchen. She liked *him.*

Brilliant, Valenti, said a voice in her head. An FBI bomb expert. Great life expectancy there. She'd be far better off with Scott, fellow cryptologist, or even Marc. Models didn't ordinarily get blown up in the line of duty.

How had she gone so far over her head with this guy without even noticing? She didn't let herself get tangled in men. She steered clear of anyone who might snare her.

And look at her. Mooning over this man.

An FBI bomb expert who was part Italian.

Who kissed exactly the way she'd always imagined Brad Pitt might, that lower lip so lusciously plump.

An FBI bomb expert with the life expectancy of a street cat, who was part Italian, who kissed like a gigolo, with eyes like neon sapphires, who *cooked*.

"I had a cat at Athena Academy," she said to distract herself.

"Yeah?"

She stuck her hands in her back pockets. "His name was Hop-A-Long because he lost a leg to a coyote when he was a kitten. Arthur, my mentor, saved him by banging the coyote on the head."

"Did the coyote die?"

"No. He dropped the kitten and ran away."

With a circular gesture, he sprinkled goat cheese over the surface of the firming eggs. "Cat's name should have been Lucky."

"He was a lifesaver for me." She stepped forward with the spatula from the counter and handed it to him. "I was pretty lonely when I first went there."

Gracefully, Lex flipped thin egg over the filling. "Hold that thought a minute. This is ready."

"Want me to lift the pan?"

"Please. This is tricky."

Together, they managed to get the omelet on the plates, and settled in to eat. Lex poured big glasses of milk. "Dig in, honey," he said.

When he sat down, she saw that he had massive circles under his eyes. "Thank you, Lex," she said. "It was very nice of you to cook. Did they give you drugs at the hospital, too?"

He nodded, displayed a bottle. "Will you open it? Childproof."

She did, and took out her own envelope. They popped their pills.

"So you were lonely at school?" he prompted.

"Oh, yeah. I forgot." She took a bite of omelet and it was very good. "Mmm. Very nice."

"Thanks. The cat. Being lonely."

Kim looked at him. Unusual that a man really did want to know something about a woman, rather than just wanting to tell all about himself. "Well, I have a big, close family—not just brothers and sisters, but cousins, aunts, uncles, everybody in the neighborhood, who know me, and my whole family—my whole history."

He smiled and nodded appreciatively.

"And then I landed in this exclusive boarding school, and I was really happy to be there, but I was pretty young for my age, and they all seemed so glamorous and together and tough." She made a soft noise. "I was very, very lonely, and Hop-A-Long helped."

"D'you have a pet now?"

"It wouldn't be fair—I'm not at home enough." Her hunger took over and she fell into eating the perfectly cooked omelet. In companionable, exhausted silence, they ate.

Dangerous, Kim thought. His kitchen, with the art deco designs in the tiles. His scent of cloves and man, which was surely the perfume of a devil or a demon. "My grandma" she said, spearing a piece of egg on her fork, "would say Sicilians are all dogs who eat out of their pans."

He chuckled. "Would she?"

"I gather this is some evil mark of culture, but I never quite got it. Why Italians would hate other Italians."

He drank his milk, nodded.

"And anyway." Kim said, "it's no secret that Nana fell in love with Johnny Bacino when she was sixteen. He was practically right off the boat from Sicily and he broke her heart." She lifted a shoulder. "So, forever after, Sicilians were dogs."

"Tough woman."

"She's that."

"Mom's mom or dad's mom?"

"My dad's." She took another bite of omelet. "This is the best omelet I've ever eaten, Lex."

"Way better than McD's, huh?"

She nodded. "My mom isn't Italian. She's Irish. My dad met her in Vietnam, brought her home."

"A nurse, right?"

For a second, Kim hesitated. It seemed she was talking an awful lot. It wasn't really like her. But what did it hurt? It wasn't as if she was telling state secrets. "Yeah, a nurse. She works oncology now."

"Vietnam to cancer. She'll get her wings in heaven, all right."

"My father wanted her to stay home, but she wouldn't hear of it. She caused wars in Baltimore's Little Italy, I can tell you. So independent and fierce, she made everybody mad."

"So you come by it honestly."

"I guess I do." She blinked, feeling the warmth of food in her belly, the comfort of finally stopping after such a long day. There was a pleasant buzz at the base of her neck, and she blinked again, more slowly.

Her body jerked, and she realized she'd very nearly keeled over right into her plate.

Lex caught her arm. "Hey, you all right?"

She stood up. "I have to go to bed right now."

In an instant, Lex was beside her. "Come on."

"I'll shower in the morning," she said, swaying as she turned toward the hallway she'd seen.

"That's fine." He took her elbow, led her down the hall and opened a door. He flipped on the light. A small bedroom with two narrow windows was revealed. The bed was covered with a green-and-white spread. The blinds were open and Kim noticed vaguely that it was still snowing. Lex moved to close them and she shook her head. "Leave them."

She sank down on the bed and started taking off her shoes. One landed with a thump. Then the other. She stripped off her socks.

Lex said, "I'll put a toothbrush in the bathroom and bring you some towels—"

He said more, but Kim was tilting sideways, and his voice melted into a meaningless wash of sound as sleep rose up and claimed her.

Chapter 10

Wednesday, October 6

Kim awakened one toe at a time. She couldn't immediately remember where she was. The bed was
deep and comfortable. She'd made a nest of pillows
and blankets around her, as was her habit, and one
foot hung over the edge of the bed.

Opening one eye, she saw an uncurtained window, with snow falling past it.

Chicago.

Oh, yeah.

Lex.

She took a breath, started to throw off the covers,

and groaned. Sore muscles cried out from every corner of her body—arms, ribs, neck. Her ear woke up
and started to throb. Kim put a hand to it. Who knew
a freaking ear could hurt so much?

With effort, she sat upright and tossed the tangles
of covers from her body. Through the window she
could see that it was still snowing, swirls of big fat
flakes. After a minute, she stood up to stretch out the
stiffness. Her ankle immediately protested, and she
limped a little as she crossed to the window to check
out the weather. She blinked. "Good grief."

It must have snowed all night. Drifts half covered
the cars parked on the street. There wasn't a soul anywhere that she could see. No traffic. It was a side
street, but it didn't look as if there'd been any cars
along the street for quite a long time.

Her clothes were wretchedly twisted and uncom-
fortable. She straightened out her bra, shook down
her jeans, thinking about how fast she'd passed out
last night. Her mouth tasted like an alien died in it.

Coffee. A shower.

The room, now that she could see it, was as mar-
velous as the rest of the house. Clean lines. Simple
stuff—blond wood with a little bit of a curve. On one
wall hung a beaux arts painting of a woman in a
green gown. A dresser, a night table and a bed were
the only furnishings. It was small, but on a bright day,
it would be very appealing.

A pile of towels was on the dresser, and Kim spied

a note on top. Lex's handwriting was spare and slanted, oddly elegant.

> Hope you slept well. There is coffee in the pot—just hit the button. Feel free to take a shower and help yourself to whatever you need. I thought you might need fresh clothes, too, so try these (would you believe they belong to my sister?). ☺ Lex.

She chuckled and picked up the clothes—a pair of yoga pants and a T-shirt. They looked as if they'd fit all right. Much better than leaving on her wrinkled, crumpled, old clothes.

Gathering everything to take with her, she padded out into the hall, dark and cool. Diamond-shaped tiles paved the length of it, dramatic in black and something lighter—maybe ivory. Light fixtures were frosted glass in the shape of fans.

What a place! It had to be worth a fortune.

She found the bathroom at the end of the hall, remembering what he'd said last night about noticing the room. It was fantastic. Ivory-colored porcelain fixtures had a carved pattern of lines around them, on the big deep bathtub, repeated in the sink and even the toilet. Wall tiles were a rich teal, edged with long, narrow rectangles of black. A divider of glass brick between the toilet and a shower area created a sense of light and space.

"Wow," she said aloud. Lex had set out a brand-new toothbrush on the sink. She unwrapped it and brushed gratefully, then turned on the taps for the shower. As the water heated, she stripped out of the old, tangled, slept-in clothes and let them fall on the floor, taking inventory as steam began to curl down from the ceiling.

Her body was definitely banged up. A bruise the size of a dahlia bloomed over her ribs and side. Her ankle was black-and-blue, swollen.

Only then did she look at her face. It wasn't as bad as she'd feared, but it wasn't pretty. There was a cut on her eyebrow where she'd hit the table in the conference room, with small black-and-blue marks around it. A bruise bloomed on her cheekbone. Her lower lip was a little swollen. A look of general weariness tugged down her features.

She lifted her hair to look at her throbbing, hot ear. Very ugly. Puffy, multicolored, laced with stitches. "Jerk," she growled, thinking of the man who had attacked her in the conference room. His face with its curiously masklike expression flashed over her memory. She shuddered.

The glass-brick shower was an open stall, and Kim felt strangely vulnerable in it, as if she were on display. And yet, it was delicious, too. His soap smelled like cloves—that's where the scent came from!—and there were good bottles of shampoo in hotel-size samples in an open-weave plastic container in one corner. The teal-and-black tiles reflected through the glass brick, danced on the water.

She washed. Thought of Lex, kissing her last night.

Thought of that luscious lower lip, his long fingers spiraling circles over her palm.

Thought of him in his bed somewhere not very far away. Did he sleep nude?

Thought of him nude, wet, here, kissing her.

She moved the water temperature to cold and let it shock her. *Quit it,* she told herself. He was way too right for her. Which made him all too wrong. She knew what happened when women fell in love with a man—little bits and pieces of them disappeared until the dreams and ambitions were memories and dust. She saw it over and over again.

After her shower, she dressed in the T-shirt and yoga pants—which left about an inch and a half of tummy uncovered—and combed out her wet hair. She left the curls to air-dry on her shoulders and wandered into the kitchen. In spite of the cloud cover, the room was light and airy feeling, with windows on two sides. A back door she'd missed last night appeared to open onto a small, rooftop patio area. Planters, empty now, were piled with snow, and a table with a closed umbrella stood by a wall.

"Jeez," she said aloud, and turned on the coffeemaker. She wondered again what the place would cost if he'd had to buy it instead of inherit. And who had been pissed to be left out of that inheritance?

As she waited for the coffee to brew, she picked up her cell phone to check for messages. It was, predictably, dead, since she'd forgotten to plug it in. And even if she'd remembered, the charger was in the backpack she'd left behind at the television station. She made a mental note to see if they could get that backpack mailed to her.

Ugh. No cell phone. No computer, no way to contact the outside world. It made her feel twitchy. A laptop sat on the counter, but she wouldn't dare open it. Not without permission. She could use a landline phone, but although she saw a modem line, she didn't see an actual telephone. Maybe it was in his bedroom or something.

Eyeing the laptop, she did have to wonder if he'd ever talked to her from this spot. It was connected via modem to the outside world.

"Good morning," he said from behind her.

Kim jumped and put a hand to her heart. "You scared me!"

"Sorry. The smell of that coffee brewing went right under my door into my head and woke me up. I had to come find it." He stood in the doorway, shirtless. Spiky short hair bristled over the top of his perfectly shaped head. A grizzling of beard covered his angular jaw. His sweats rode low on his hips, showing a part of his lower abdomen, and it was slightly round, taut.

She looked away. "It's almost ready."

"Cups in that cupboard right above the coffee-maker there. I'll be right back."

From the cupboard, she took two hefty mugs, black with purple interior, and set one on the counter for Lex. The other she filled midstream from the pot, unable to wait.

She wanted him to be wearing a shirt when he came back.

He wasn't.

And if he'd looked good to her in a photo, or dressed in a leather jacket last night, or standing outside the hospital, his head dotted with snow—well, it all paled by comparison. Shoulders, hard and round; chest scattered with exactly the right amount of dark hair, silkily and artfully spread between his dark nipples; that smooth belly.

She aimed for a disdainfully arched brow. "Go put some clothes on, Luthor. You're half-naked."

He touched his chest with his good palm. "Making you nervous?"

Snow light caught along one rib. Kim wanted to taste the round line with her tongue. "No," she said.

"Liar," he said with a smile in his voice.

Kim met his eyes. "It would just be a bad idea."

His eyes, even sleepy, were electrically blue. "*What* would be?" He stepped closer, and Kim found her back against the counter. His gaze moved down her face, lingered at her mouth, moved lower. It felt as if he were touching her, and in reaction, her hips softened. She forced herself not to react, not to do anything but meet his eyes with a steely glance of her own.

"Having sex," she said, and was pleased by how level she sounded.

"Maybe I was just thinking about kissing you," he said.

"No, you weren't. And anyway, that's probably not a good idea, either."

"Oh, well," he murmured.

And did it anyway.

It was so smooth, so easy that Kim couldn't even bristle. One minute he was standing in front of her, the next he bent fluidly and slanted his mouth over hers and kissed her. She winced a little, and he whispered, "Sorry," then more gently kissed her. His whole body seemed to take part, coaxing her body into it. His mouth opened and invited her to come exploring. His hands moved slowly on her back, which she discovered was arched, pressing her bare lower belly into the bareness of his lower belly, and he noticed it, too, and moved, back and forth. A large, lazy snake of an erection rose and nudged into her thighs. Kim made a soft noise.

"Kissing is good, hmm?" he said, and bent his head lower, to kiss her neck. Lazy hot tongue coiling circles around her throat, lazy hand curling up her body, lazy nudging of his cock against her leg.

It was crazy, but he felt really good. He smelled

exactly right, too, and his tongue, moving on her throat, made a ripple of arousal rise up her spine. He slid his hand beneath the shirt, stroked her side. "Should I stop?"

"Probably."

"You'll have to sound more definite than that, sweetheart."

His hand rose beneath her shirt, hot, smooth palm sliding up her side, her ribs, heading upward for the breasts that were primed and tingling in anticipation of the contact of bare palm, nude fingers. Instead of pulling away, as she sensibly should have, Kim found herself pressing closer.

He moved with deliberate laziness. *Slow hands,* Kim thought, and welcomed the touch of his full lips when he raised his head to kiss her again. His tongue swirled into her mouth, his fingers teased her nipples to fierce points, and he rubbed closer to her thigh.

Kim touched his erection, stroking it with her fingers, testing the size and heft of it. "Very nice," she whispered, and he was kissing her again, deep and long.

"It's all yours, honey."

He slid his hands beneath her T-shirt, pushed it upward and Kim lifted her arms to let him take it off, glad when he made a cheered and satisfied sound over her breasts. Delighted when he bent his big head and sucked a nipple into his mouth. He knew how to do that right, too, slow and probing, then a little harder.

It was crazy. It was too fast. She had to sometimes work with this guy, but she didn't care. She wanted him. Now, today, this minute.

A sound like a ping or a rubber band or something—

"What—?"

Lex knocked her sideways and something crashed on the counter behind her. The glass in the kitchen door shattered into the room. Kim hit the floor, covering her head and eyes instinctively.

"Stay down!" Lex yelled, and scrambled, crablike, across the kitchen floor.

Kim stayed plastered to the floor for a few seconds, her hands over her head. The tile floor was cold on her naked torso, and she felt her ear begin to throb again. Another bullet blazed into the kitchen and slammed into the tiles near the door to the hallway. Absurdly, Kim felt protectively furious over the beauty of the apartment and wanted the shooting to stop before it hurt something precious.

She sized up the direction of the shooting, then scrambled behind the island where they'd been sitting last night. "Can you see the shooter?"

Lex, plastered along the kitchen wall, peered through the door. "Can't see anything through the snow. Gotta be right across the street, though. There's nothing else."

"Or he's right *on* the roof."

"Snow is deep. We'd be able to see footsteps."

Without her shirt, Kim felt exposed and foolish. The T-shirt lay where Lex had dropped it a few minutes before, on the threshold to the other room, a good twelve feet away. Huddling beneath the lip of the counter, she crossed her arms over her breasts, but it wasn't much help. Flesh spilled over, and she still felt stupid, crouching beneath the table, half-naked.

In sudden decision, she scrambled over the floor toward the counter—

Bullets pinged into the room over her head, so close she heard the whiz across her skin.

"Valenti!"

Kim swore and dived back to the safety of the breakfast bar. She glared at Lex, who was, she had to admit, also half-naked. It wasn't quite the same. His injured right hand was held close against his chest, and he was reaching into the drawer with his left and pulled out a revolver.

Another shot zinged into the room. He slammed back against the wall and squatted. "They have to be on the roof. Direct line of sight into the room from the roof across the street." He had the gun in his hand and squatted to send it spinning across the floor toward Kim. "You're going to have to see if you can get a shot from the window over there. I can't shoot left-handed."

Keeping one arm over her breasts, Kim picked up the gun.

"Jesus, Valenti. Stop trying to cover yourself and see if you can get this guy."

She glared at him.

"I won't look."

"Fine." It wasn't like she looked bad naked, anyway. Cocking the gun, she edged around the island and into the shadows, out of sight of the back door. There was a window over the sink, and creeping along the counter, she could probably see out without being seen.

Cautiously, she moved low to the ground and paused in front of the sink, then lifted herself slowly until she could see out of the bottom of the window. The snow was lighter, but it was still hard to tell. "I can't see anything," she said.

"The angle is a little sharper. Edge to your right a little bit."

Kim eased her body to the right, gun at the ready. "Thought you weren't looking," she said, her eyes on the horizon.

"Not at your breasts."

"Liar," she said, and halted. Was that a head? It moved, and a bullet pinged into the kitchen through the door. Kim straightened, steadied her hands, and fired through the window.

"Yeah!" The target went down. "Gotcha you son of a bitch!"

Lex bolted out the door, and Kim held her position as he dashed out into the knee-deep snow, his back bare, his black head shining in the quiet snow light.

No shots rang out. Kim stayed where she was, arms straight and ready to fire, until he waved an arm. All clear. Keeping her eyes on the window her bullet had broken, she felt along the counter for her T-shirt. Remembered it was on the floor, and she turned, careful not to step in broken glass with her bare feet, and picked up the shirt.

Lex came in behind her, and she tucked the shirt around her breasts. Dots of snow hung in his hair, and his shoulders were wet. "They're gone."

Kim clicked the safety into place and lowered the gun. "I'm pretty sure I got somebody."

"Yeah. There are reinforcements on the way."

"Good."

His eyes were hot and blue as he reached out and took hold of the T-shirt. Kim resisted for a moment, then let it go, dropping her arms.

"Now I'm looking," he said, holding the shirt in his hand. He didn't touch her, and Kim felt a ripple down her back that pulled her shoulder blades down, lifted her breasts higher.

"I see that," she said.

"You have the most beautiful breasts I've ever seen." His nostrils flared. "Can we start over?"

She lifted the gun. "Not until this is evened up a bit."

He raised his hands in mock fear. "What do you want, darlin'?" That elegantly arched eyebrow lifted. "Your wish is my command."

"Lose the sweats."

"I might be a teeny bit aroused, darlin'."

Kim blinked, slowly. "All the better."

Lex skimmed the sweats off his body and kicked them aside, and lifted his hands to the sides, as if to say, "There it is."

Beautiful, she thought. That lower belly, so taut and smooth, curving down to a very aroused appendage. She moved forward, put the gun on the counter, and touched it. It leaped a little, and she smiled. "Nice."

"Glad you approve, darlin'."

"We don't have time to have sex, you know," she said, and her heart was pounding as she stroked the silky casing.

"I know." He bent his head and captured one nipple in his hot mouth. He rolled it, hard, across his tongue, and Kim made a noise.

"Maybe if we did it very fast," she whispered.

"No, baby," he said, putting his naked body against hers, yanking her hips to his. In a very low, quiet, gravelly voice he said, "We're going to have the best, hottest, longest, sexiest sex either one of us has ever had."

"When?"

He rolled her nipple between his fingers, ran his tongue along her lower lip. "Not today."

She didn't want to wait. He filled her head like a

fog, and she stroked his cock, reached lower and cupped him in her hand. "After the police come?"

"No." His tongue moved on her mouth, into her mouth, and his hands were on her breasts, weighing them, thumbs brushing over her nipples. "I think we have to wait at least a week or two."

Her tailbone was melting, she'd swear it was, and she could feel that he was trembling with desire. "Why?"

"Because anticipation is worth it."

"Okay," she said, and backed away. "Remember, though. You're the one who said it."

He rested vivid eyes on her face, and Kim saw something flash there. Heat, yes. Desire, absolutely. But something else, too. Richer, deeper, warmer. "I'm not gonna make it easy for you to just walk away from me," he said.

"Why would I walk away?"

"Because," he said with a little smile as he climbed back into his sweats, "that's what you do."

Kim pulled the shirt over her head. There wasn't really an answer. "Better call your boys. I'm going to go get dressed." She paused. "See if somebody has a charger for a Sanyo phone."

Chapter 11

The streets in the main part of the city were much clearer than they were on the side streets, so it was only an hour before the FBI crew arrived. Lex had already gone across the street to the roof opposite his apartment, and although he found footsteps and a smear of blood, the shooter had disappeared.

"Any clues to who it might be?" Kim asked when he returned. She paused in the act of sweeping up shattered glass from the tiny tiles in the kitchen.

"Obviously, they figured out who I am." He lifted a shoulder. "I'm guessing it's the same group. If there's a DNA match in the national database, we'll know more."

He displayed the sample of red snow he'd picked up in a cup.

When the rest of the crew arrived, they brought with them Kim's things, and she was relieved to be able to put on her own clothes. After the discussion of this morning's shooter, a short, blocky man asked Kim if she'd talk to him about the events last evening. She gave him as much detail as she was able about everything.

At the end, he said, "What led you to the television station, anyway? We didn't pick up on that at all."

"Tip," Kim said simply, and shrugged. "A good one, obviously, so I'd like to protect my source."

The man nodded, flipped his notebook closed.

Lex and his compatriots measured and taped and tapped the scene. Kim felt impatient, but the news of the weather was grim: the airport was shut down, which meant there was no point in trying to get out of Chicago today. The city phone lines were jammed, but Kim finally got her cell phone to operate and caught Scott at NSA headquarters. "Shepherd here."

"Hey, Scott. It's me."

"Damn, Valenti, what'd I tell you about playing maverick, huh?"

"It's not like I had a choice. Once the terrorists overran the television station, I pretty much had to do whatever I could to get out."

"I know. You looked like hell on the news this

morning, though. Pissed off, too, huh? You were pretty rude to those reporters."

It was one thing that her mother had seen her last night, because the senior Valenti had been trolling for information. "What news did you see?"

"Honey, you were on every national news program in the country. I saw you on CNN, but Mary and Jo saw you on *Good Morning America*."

Kim couldn't think of anything to say. "I'm sorry, Scott. It must seem like I'm grandstanding. You worked just as hard as I did to crack this code."

"C'mon, you know me better than that. I know *you* better than that."

"Ugh." She rubbed the spot between her eyebrows and realized suddenly that she still really didn't feel all that great. "I'll get out of here tomorrow, but in the meantime, we should stay on this. Mansour got away, and he's obviously the ringleader. Another guy we need to find out about is a creepy dude who slammed me into a table a few dozen times."

"I'm on it. Mansour is the one who lead the siege at the station last night. He's been tangled up in arms deals and a few other things over the past decade. I'm bringing up all kinds of interesting links."

Kim realized there were a half-dozen FBI agents standing around, pretending not to listen. "Whatever you do," Kim said, with a grin in their direction, "the FBI in Chicago is out of the loop."

"Ha, ha, ha," said an agent standing nearby, a

burly blonde who'd have given Scott a run for his money in the Adonis department.

Casually, she moved toward the living room and looked out the window. "I don't think they're done yet, and we probably need to check Columbus Day connections—parades, celebrations, whatever."

"Columbus Day?" Scott echoed with skepticism. "Yeah, if the terrorists were Native American, maybe."

Kim made up a lie to cover her Oracle connection. "I overheard them talking about Columbus Day. And there have been moving vans stolen."

"All right."

"And you know, anti-American sentiment might lend itself well to Columbus Day, if you think about it. It commemorates the discovery of America, right? Not quite as patriotic as Fourth of July or anything, but not out of the realm."

"I'll see what I can find out."

"Thanks. I'm sure I'll get on a plane in the morning. I'll call and let you know."

A short pause on the other end of the line. "Are you still with that guy?" Scott asked.

"What guy?" Kim asked.

"The one with you at the airport last night."

"Yeah. They hustled me out of the reporters' spotlights. I'm safe."

Another noisy pause.

"What?" Kim prompted.

"Can you go in another room or something?"

She raised her brows. "Sure." She carried the phone into the bedroom she'd slept in last night. "Okay. I'm alone. What's up?"

"Are you really okay?"

"Well, I had my ass kicked last night, and somebody tried to kill us this morning, but other than that, yeah, everything's fine."

"He's not hustling you, is he?"

"Shepherd, cut the caveman thing, all right? I'm not your girl, and it's never been like that between us. Don't even go there."

"I'm not. I wasn't." He cleared his throat. "Just worried about you."

"That's sweet, but I can take care of myself."

"I know."

"Look, I'll talk to you tomorrow, okay?"

"Yep. If you want a ride, let me know."

Kim frowned. "I left my car at the airport, but thanks."

When she hung up, she stared at the phone for a long moment. Had she missed signals from her partner? It would be a shame to have to break up this partnership. It worked very well.

No. He was just being a guy. Lex probably threatened a lot of men.

A whispered memory went through her mind: *We're going to have the best, hottest, longest, sexiest sex either one of us has ever had.*

But not today. And that, in her opinion, was a

very good thing. She thought she might have too many aches and pains, for one thing. For another, he was flat-out dangerous to her peace of mind.

She was going to have one hot affair with Lex Tanner, there was no question about that.

But she had to be careful how it progressed, or her carefully guarded heart was going to be snared right along with her body.

Once the mess had been cleaned up, and nearly everyone had gone—except the guard stationed outside, Kim and Lex were left alone in his beautiful apartment. Her things were delivered and it seemed the worst might be over for the moment.

He turned on the television. "You look beat, Valenti," he said. "Let's find an old movie to watch and make some sandwiches, what d'you say?"

The idea was unexpectedly welcome. Kim rubbed the spot between her brows that held tension. "That sounds good, but I'm wondering if you'd mind if I got online for a few minutes, just to check a couple of leads."

"Not at all, especially if you share them." He glared at the taped-over window, where a cold breeze tried to push inside. "Let's go to my office. Much warmer."

Kim padded behind him, bundled in a sweater and socks. "What do you think is going to happen next?"

He lifted a shoulder. "Considering the elections are only a couple of weeks, I'd say it's safe to predict violence somewhere along this continuum, wouldn't you?"

"Yeah. The trouble is, where? When? With what?"

"Damn terrorists," Lex drawled. "So unpredictable. Can't they get a planned agenda, like any decent criminal?"

"Very funny. You have any bright ideas, smart guy?"

"Sit," he said, pulling out a green leather office chair on rollers. Like the rest of the apartment, there was a thirties bohemian flair to this room. Rolltop desk, made of oak, shelves filled with books, a stained-glass lamp.

"Now this room looks like you," Kim said.

"And this is a room," he said with an inclination of his head, "that I indeed furnished myself. It used to be her parlor."

"You've got good taste, Luthor."

He winked. "You better believe it. Now, I'll leave you alone. Internet icon to the left there."

"Thanks. Not everyone likes sharing a computer."

"I got nothing to hide, sweetheart. And you don't strike me as a snoopy weird woman, either."

"You never know."

He was on his way out. "Oh, yeah, you do. I've got excellent instincts."

Kim signed on to the network, then pulled up her personal files. If Scott found anything between now and the time she got home, he'd send it here. She'd also be able to track some of her work e-mails.

But the important thing was to check the Oracle. It was dicey to sign in through a remote server, but she went to AA.gov and slipped through a back door and electronically "knocked."

A white box popped up.

DELPHI: Who's there?

Kim responded with a formalized script:

VISITOR: Ariadne
VISITOR: Password: Hop-A-Long
VISITOR: Weight, 117
VISITOR: Arabic, French, Spanish, Navajo
VISITOR: NSA

Kim waited for a moment. The box closed and a second one opened, and she went through the same dance with no prompts. The box closed, and a third one opened, this one a soft blue.

DELPHI: Good job, Ariadne. We saw you on the news.

VISITOR: I had a lot of help, but thanks. Now what? Any more info?

DELPHI: Mansour escaped the television station along with an arms dealer named Richard Dunst.

VISITOR: Someone tried to kill me this morning. So there is still a plot afoot.

DELPHI: We have no clues at this time.

VISITOR: Was the footage of the CIA dealer selling arms to Keminis a true one?

DELPHI: Unfortunately, yes.

VISITOR: Thanks.

DELPHI: Reporters will be panting like dogs, Ariadne. Be cagey.

VISITOR: Will do.

Signing out of the live communication, Kim went to the Web site for her home service and signed in to check e-mails on her personal account very quickly. There were two from her mother and four from her sisters. Kim wrote short notes to each of them:

I'm safe. Love you lots. See you this weekend for supper and the parade, okay?

She shut down the browser, went to the history functions to erase her steps, and ran a quick check to be sure he had no key-recording software. None that was known, which was the best you could ever do. The passwords and script were changed if she used them even once, so they were safe anyway, but it was always better to be cautious.

When she wandered out of the office, she found Lex in the kitchen, pressing wood putty into one of the bullet holes. "I'll get the glass replaced tomorrow," he said. "But some of these holes are going to be tough to fix."

"I was very worried about your beautiful apartment," Kim said, talking an olive out of the bowl on the counter.

"Were you?"

She laughed. "Crazy, huh?"

"A bit."

They loaded a tray with pickles, more cracked olives, cubes of cheese and the not-quite-as-fresh-as-it-could-be half of a French loaf, and some wheat crackers, and carried it all into the living room.

"I'm afraid to eat on that couch," Kim said, eyeing the shimmery, velvety grain.

"Yeah, it's fancy-shmancy," Lex agreed, munching on a pickle, "But I have it outsmarted." He lifted the top of a table and took out a pink-and-green striped sheet. Shaking it out, he tossed it over the couch. "Voilà!"

"Cool." Kim collapsed happily, and made a plate to balance on her thighs. The ottomans were big and comfortable, the pillows just right for creating nests.

"I've never been to a guy's house that had such comfortable stuff."

"Well, these things came with the apartment, but I've always prided myself on comfortable. My old couch was really great."

"But I bet it was plaid. Brown plaid or orange plaid or red microfiber." She lifted a finger. "No. Leather. You might be a leather kind of guy."

"You're gonna have to work on your little problem with stereotypes, girl."

"Yeah?"

"Yeah. It was kinda soft stuff—dark blue, for your information, with white-striped pillows." Only he said it "pillas," which cracked her up. "What?"

"Nothing."

"You don't believe me?"

"I do," she said. "You're right. I do stereotype men. But most of you deserve it."

"You've just been hanging around those Washington types too much. Too many politicians and law enforcement folks."

"And what are you, if you're not law enforcement?"

"I'm the bomb squad, man!" He said it with an exaggerated drawl, and popped an olive in his mouth. "I'm bad. I'm cool. I'm *all* that."

Kim laughed. "Yeah, yeah, whatever." He flipped through channels, pausing for reasons Kim couldn't discern, racing through when she would have halted. "How'd you end up on the bomb squad, anyway?"

He wiggled his stocking feet. Clicked the remote. "I was a firebug as a kid. I got in trouble a couple of times, and the sheriff was gonna lock me up, but a judge put me in a probationary program for restless kids."

"Ah, so you discovered the good in your evil?"

"Not exactly." The cat jumped up on the couch and plopped down between them, purring loudly. "I ran into a kid who built bombs. Better than fire."

"Good grief."

"Yeah, that's what my mama thought. She yanked me right out of there, put me in this weird school in the Blue Ridge Mountains where everybody's parents were hippies, and I'd have done anything to get out of there, so I promised I'd never set another fire or plant a bomb again, and I didn't."

"Thank God."

He tapped his forehead. "The bomb stuff stuck, though."

"And so did the organic eating. You said it was your mother."

"It was. She was a Chicago hippie, went down South to reform it or something, and met my daddy, who was already reformed, and fell madly in love with her right on the spot. Took her a little while to fall back the other way."

"Are they both still alive?"

"Yep. Along with three sisters who spoiled me rotten."

"Mmm. Now that doesn't surprise me in the slightest."

He took her hand. "Hey, now. Be nice."

Kim gently slid her hand out of his grasp. "I am. But you can't hold my hand right now. I'm too tired and cranky."

He chuckled and leaned back against the couch. "Me, too." He flipped channels, and abruptly sat up. "Hey, look! There you are!"

The grainy video showed a man with a rifle standing guard at the UBC station, and Kim dropping suddenly out of the ceiling to his shoulders. She subdued the gunman, then bent over and took his pistol. When she stood up, there was blood on her face, trickling from her eyebrow and lips, but smearing her neck and chest.

"Eww," she cried. "That's gross! Why do they keep showing it over and over again?"

"Because, sweetheart," he drawled, "you look very tough and very hot."

Kim rolled her eyes. "Please."

"It's true. Not a man out there who isn't thinkin', hey, that's my kind of girl."

"Girl?"

He cut her a mischievous look.

Kim let it pass.

"How'd you learn to do so much, anyway?"

"The Athena Academy," she said simply.

"I've heard of that. The school for girls in Arizona?"

Kim raised her eyebrows. "You've really heard of it?"

"It's been in the news a little bit lately, hasn't it? A murder."

"Oh. Yeah. Very sad stuff."

Lex looked at her intently. "How is it different, this school?"

Kim chuckled. "In every possible way. I had to learn languages, weapons, survival training, as well as maths and sciences."

His eyebrow arched in a way that was becoming familiar. "Is that where you learned Arabic?"

She nodded. "It's an interesting place, established by a woman who wanted to see other women be placed in high positions through the government—and she found ways to discover the most talented women—" she gestured toward herself with one arched brow "—such as myself, and bring them to the Academy to be educated."

"You are very talented," he said.

"Thank you." With a shift of one shoulder, she went on, "In that environment, I was very ordinary. The women who are recruited are extremely intelligent, athletic and always talented in some specific way. They search everywhere for these women."

"And besides becoming cryptographers, what do they do?"

"A lot of things. Tory Patton is an Athena grad."

"The reporter?"

"Yep. One of my friends, Diana, is with army intelligence, and our friend Selena works for the CIA. She's married now, but I still see her."

"Does marriage interfere with friendship?"

"Sometimes."

He leaned his head against the couch and looked at her. The jeweled eyes were shadowed, exhausted, and Kim knew she must look the same way. "You're pretty cool, Valenti," he said.

"You, too, Luthor." Impulsively, she bent over and kissed his very kissable mouth. "I think I could like you."

His smile was slow and liquid. "Oh, honey, you'll like me. I guarantee it."

"Don't be so arrogant, Tanner."

He bent his head and touched his nose to her shoulder, a gesture that caught Kim off guard. It was tender and somehow boyish. "I'm not arrogant. We're just a good match, that's all."

"How can you possibly know that in one day?"

He picked up her hand, saying. "Just for purposes of illustration, all right? Don't get testy on me."

His palm was hard and smooth, and she didn't have any desire to take her hand away. "All right," she said. "I'm listening."

"Look how our hands fit together."

"That doesn't mean anything."

"What about this?" he said, and leaned in closer to her mouth. "Can I kiss you?"

"Yes," she whispered.

"See, our mouths," he said so close to her lips that she felt the shaping of the words, "are exactly right." He pressed in, closed the space between their lips. His upper went between her upper and lower; her lower was sandwiched between his. His lips were plump but not squishy, firm but not too hard. He kissed close, then let her go, then kissed again. "See?" ·

"Yes," Kim whispered.

"And if I," he said, still kissing her in between words, "put my hand up here on your face, like this—" he cupped her jaw, his long fingers shaping themselves to her cheekbone, the tips resting near her eye "—then it adds something for both of us."

"You should stop this," she whispered.

"Probably," he agreed, but didn't. He just kept kissing her softly, just using his lips, soft and firm. Tender. Little plucking kisses, tight little nibbles of suction on her lower lip, with just a hint of teeth behind, his fingers exploring gently.

Kim relaxed under the sweetness and lifted her own hand to his face. Lean, chiseled, edges of bone strong beneath her fingertips.

"Wow," he said, not pulling away, his eyes closed. "Wow."

Kim felt herself drifting into his touch, falling under a spell that would leave her weak and sleeping right next to him all night long in this dangerously seductive apartment on a snowy autumn evening.

Not good.

She pulled back, all the way. Stood up, moved away. "Sorry," she said, pushing her hair from her face. She was aware that she must look quite aroused, her face flushed, her nipples standing at attention beneath the soft T-shirt. "I don't want to do this now. Not tonight. We're too—"

Lex was on his feet. "Shh. It's okay, honey. I'm sorry." His hands were on her shoulders, soothing, easing. "It's okay," he repeated. "Let's sit down and watch movies. I promise I won't do anything else."

"We're tired. I don't trust emotions going crazy under these circumstances."

"You're right." He patted her arms, which was an oddly reassuring gesture, and went back to the couch. "I'll build a pillow wall, okay?"

Kim laughed softly.

"C'mon," he said, cocking his beautiful head. "You're safe, Valenti. I promise. Let's just watch TV."

She sat down.

Chapter 12

Thursday, October 7

Kim supposed she should have been prepared for the siege of reporters, but she wasn't. They were lying in wait when they emerged from his building the next morning, pushing microphones and cameras into their faces.

"What's next for Q-group?"

"Pretty new girlfriend you've got there, Lex!"

"You have any leads on Mansour?"

"How'd you break the code, Kim?"

"Is the romance between the two of you heating up?"

"How does it feel to be a hero?"

Kim elbowed through, but the last question irked her. She glanced at Lex, and he nodded. She halted. "First of all, I haven't done anything by myself. There's been a team of various agents working on this problem for weeks. My partner at NSA, Scott Shepherd, was instrumental in breaking the code, and Alex Tanner—" she gestured to him "—disarmed the bomb at the airport. I'm not the hero," she said firmly. "That's all."

"Ms. Valenti, I appreciate your modesty," said a young woman, and Kim paused, simply seeing a hungry young reporter, her own counterpart, "but your courage at the television station is well documented."

Kim shook her head. "I've been trained. Like a soldier or police officer, I was just doing my job."

"Like your brother Jason?" said a male voice, booming into the fray.

"My brother was far braver than I'll ever be," Kim said with frost in her voice. "But this has nothing to do with him."

"So you don't want to get revenge on the terrorists who killed your brother?"

Lex started to move between her and the reporter, who was obviously pleased at hitting a soft spot. Kim waved Lex back and met the reporter's gaze. "If you don't get anything else from this clip, get this," she said in hard tones. "An eye for an eye doesn't work. If I want to kill terrorists for killing my brother, then I'm no better than they are. We're trying to prevent violence, not add to it. And last night, that's what we did."

The reporters roared, but Kim ducked into the car without any further comment.

"Well done," Lex said in the car.

Grimly, Kim looked at him. "Not really. I've just invited a thousand reporters to pursue me for quotes."

He winked. "You can handle it." As the car pulled neatly through the parting bodies, he added, "You might want to come up with a few pat statements. This isn't going to go away for a while."

"Good suggestion. Thanks."

The car dropped Lex off at the FBI offices first. "Well," he said, "this is my stop."

"Looks like it," Kim said with a faint smile.

"I'd really like to kiss you," he said, quietly, so only she could hear, "but we don't want to add any fuel to the fire."

"I'm kissing you now," she said, and met his eyes.

Vividly blue eyes, full of a mercurial glitter and heat. "I *will* be in touch," he drawled, "and I do mean in *touch*."

"Go," she said. "Here come some more reporters."

And in fact, she ran into reporters twice more before she made it safely inside the NSA offices—at both the Chicago and the Baltimore airports, she had to wave her way through gnats of them. It was easier at Chicago, where she discovered she was a VIP who was whisked through security, directly to the gate, and settled into first class on the airplane.

"Nice," she said to the attendant who brought her a cup of coffee and a newspaper.

"The airport is very grateful, Ms. Valenti."

Settling into the thick, wide seat, Kim smiled to herself. There were worse things than first class. Was this just a one-shot deal? She hoped it would last a little while. Where could she go that she'd always wanted to visit and hadn't because the flight was too awful? New Zealand! Yes.

She smiled to herself. If only she could take the time.

Her cell phone was recharged, and while she waited for the plane to board, she called Scott. "Hey," she said when he answered his desk phone. "I rethought your offer of meeting me at the airport. Reporters have been crawling all over me."

"I'll be there. When do you land?"

"One o'clock this afternoon. Have you picked up any other details or information since yesterday?"

"I'll fill you in when you arrive."

He sounded odd. "Is everything okay, Scott?"

"Sure." Which meant no.

"I guess we'll talk about that when I land, too."

"Nothing to talk about."

"Whatever you say. I'll see you in a couple of hours."

She gazed out the window as they flew, watching snow-blanketed fields and forests move into view, then out. It felt as if something had changed in her life during this brief period of hours. Was it the test of her physicality? She'd been well trained, but had never been forced to fight hand-to-hand before. In spite of the battering her body had taken, she was exhilarated at the feeling of power it gave her. She'd faced men several times her size and managed to not only hold her own, but get away and vanquish one of them.

She thought of her brother Jason. Saw him, in her mind's eye, giving her a thumbs-up. Reporters be damned, she thought. Her truly private thoughts couldn't be touched.

And what thoughts would those be? a voice said in her mind.

Kim resolutely stared at the wintry landscape and refused to think of Lex Tanner with his beautiful eyes and beautiful body and hot, hot ways.

She wondered how long it would be before she would see him again.

Kim counted her blessings that no one without a boarding pass was allowed to enter the gate areas these days. It meant she went unaccosted until she hit the baggage claim area, and there was sturdy, blond Scott, burly enough to be a bodyguard. "Hey, gorgeous," she said. "Thanks for picking me up."

He scowled, touched her forehead. "You really took a beating."

She shrugged. "I'm all right."

"Whatever you say, sweetheart. I've got a car outside—do you want a ride to yours? I can help fend off the crowds."

"Perfect." It would also give her a chance to set the record straight.

The crowd of reporters was waiting outside the airport, and Kim wondered how they knew to be there. Was it like ants or bees or something, some subvocal method of communication? How did they know where and when to show up?

"Kim, we hear you acted without orders to go to Chicago. Tell us about that."

"Is it true there was a breakdown of communication between agencies?"

"Kim, can you give us the inside on the breach between the NSA and the FBI on this case?"

She paused on the sidewalk. "I'll answer a few questions," she said, "then you gotta let me get back to work." She pointed to a woman wearing a slim gray suit with red piping.

"Ms. Valenti, can you talk about the communication problems between agencies?"

"There was no breakdown," she said distinctly. "My partner, Scott Shepherd—" she pulled him by the arm to stand next to her "—and I cracked the code and we decided to check out some things in

Chicago, just in case. As you know, we worked smoothly with the FBI once I got there." She looked at the group. "Next? You."

A youthful man stepped forward. "Do either of you have any inkling of what the terrorists are planning next?"

Pleased that Scott had been included, Kim gestured for him to answer. He said simply, "They're terrorists. That means they do the unpredictable. We have some intelligence, but we're not at liberty to share that just now."

His cell phone went off, as if on cue, and he put his hand on Kim's back. "Sorry, we gotta go."

A little tangle of roared questions followed, but they ducked out and got into Scott's car. "Nice," Kim said. And something about the word made her think of Lex. A sensory snapshot of his long, devilish kisses last night wound through her mind. A sudden, narcotic sensuality burned through her chest, pooled at the base of her spine. How did he do that? How had he washed into her mind like that?

Scott put the car in gear. "You, too." He glanced at her. "Jeez, what put that look on your face? I don't think it's me, though I wouldn't mind it."

She made an effort to clear her features. "What are you talking about?"

"Nothing." He joined traffic. "The boss wants to see you the minute you get in. I already got yelled at for letting you go alone—not that I had any choice—but you're going to hear about it, too."

"Scott, are you pissed at me?"

He turned into the long-term parking area. "Where's your car?"

She directed him to the right section. "Answer me."

"It's not pissed off, Valenti." He turned, followed the row to the end, turned again. In front of her car, he paused and looked at her. "It's just that I've been waiting for you to wake up and notice that there's somebody right in front of you who'd try just about anything to get your attention, and you fly to Chicago and fall in love."

"Who?" she said with a scowl, and at the stoniness of his handsome face, she opened her mouth. Closed it. Said, "You?"

He glanced at her. Said nothing.

"I'm sorry, Scott. I never picked up on that at all."

"I don't want to talk about it right now."

"You're the one who brought it up."

He glanced in the rearview mirror. "We're gonna hold up traffic."

She opened the passenger-side door. "Let's go have a margarita later, huh?"

He nodded.

She slammed the door and stomped over to her car. Men. Honestly!

Chapter 13

As Kim came into the office, a gaggle of her co-workers cheered. They stood up at their desks and clapped, whistled, whooped. Kim rolled her eyes, tried to wave them down, then—when they wouldn't stop—she took an exaggerated bow. "Thank you." She looked for Scott, but he wasn't in the room.

Her superior, Grant Long, a trim, sixtyish man with silver hair, gave her a smile as she entered his office. "Scott said you wanted to see me, sir."

"Come in, Kim. Sit down." He folded his hands gravely, and she felt a ripple of nervousness as she settled in a gray leather office chair. "First of all," he said, peering at her face, "how are you? You look pretty battered."

"It looks worse than it feels," she said. "I'm well trained. I can hold my own."

"I know your history has lent you a certain cachet in some circles, Valenti. And you should be proud of your background at the Athena Academy. But—"

"Sir, I'd just like to explain that there wasn't really time to—"

"Agent Valenti, you're one of the best code breakers I've got, but you have got to learn to go through channels."

"I honestly tried, sir. I called Agent Milosovich at the CIA. He wouldn't take me seriously—"

Long shook his head. "No excuses, Valenti. You know better. Everything breaks down if you don't follow the chain of command."

"What was I supposed to—"

"Follow the chain of command," he repeated.

"I see." Stung, Kim glanced away for a moment, thinking of all the lives that had been saved by her actions, and the cost she'd paid personally in physical injury. It wasn't that she felt that she was better than anyone else, just that sometimes, "proper channels" didn't move fast enough.

Trying not to show her resentment or hurt, she raised her head. "You're right, sir. I'm sorry. In the future, I'll pay more attention to protocol."

"My eye you will." He stood, and Kim stood with

him. "You'll get in over your head one of these days. You very nearly did this time."

Kim bowed her head. "It was a real possibility," she said, and met his eyes. "But I believe in what I'm doing, sir."

"I know you do." He held out his hand. "Good work, Valenti."

She took a breath, accepted the handshake. "Thank you, sir."

"There is one more thing," he said, not letting her go.

"Yes, sir."

"You've been promoted. Congratulations."

Her eyes flew open. "Really?"

He grinned. "It was excellent work, distinguishing you from your peers brilliantly."

Kim thought of Scott. "And my partner?"

"Er...no. Not yet. You're being recognized for independent action. And probably because the case is so visible."

"I see."

"He's an excellent agent. No worries. He'll move up in no time."

"But he's still my partner, right?"

"Yes, ma'am."

Kim nodded. "Well, thank you, sir. Very much. I'm honored."

"You're welcome. Now go see if you can find Mansour before he plants another bomb somewhere."

"I'm on it."

The first thing she did was find Scott. He was in the copy room, peering at a page of tiny code, shaking his head, and Kim knew how to find him by the way a girl in the secretarial pool was mooning toward the open door.

"Shepherd," she said. "Mama's tonight? My treat since you covered my ass so well."

His lips turned down happily. "Yeah. I'll go for that. Come here and take a look at this. I think we've got a variation of the e-mail virus happening here. See what you think."

Kim took the sheaf of papers. It was e-mails in Arabic, once again, but Scott had highlighted some imbedded code. "I think you're right," she said. "Let's get on it."

"Cool."

She gave him back the papers and said, "You know, the blonde at the end over there has been sighing over you for six weeks. Maybe you ought to put her out of her misery and ask her out."

His mouth quirked up at the corners. "Implying what, Valenti?"

She spread her hands. "Come to your own conclusions, babe," she said.

He went to the door. "The blonde on the end?"

"The very one."

"She's gorgeous, but maybe a little too young for me."

Kim winked. "She's twenty-five. Just looks young." She slapped his arm with the papers. "I'll leave you to it."

Mama Rosa's was a storefront trattoria in suburban Washington, D.C., not far from the job. Kim had discovered it shortly after coming to the NSA and loved it for the traditional Italian foods she missed—she could feast here without having to deal with the hassle of family. It was agreeably low lit, with snowy tablecloths and plenty of bread and the smell of roasting garlic mixed with basil thick in the air.

Kim breathed in the scent deeply. It smelled of home. Of raviolis and fresh affection and hearty food. Even Mama—aka Rosalie—who hurried forward when she spied them at the door, could have been an auntie with her lush bosom and pretty shoes. God forbid comfort should come before sex appeal when it came to shoes. Kim eyed the black, high-heeled sandals with something akin to awe. Rosalie had to spend ten hours a day on her feet.

The woman swept them both into an affectionate wave of perfume and oregano, giving them a beneficent smile before she realized Kim was a little battered. "Baby! What happened to you?"

Kim waved a hand. "Oh, you know. Work."

"You shouldn't be working at such job," she said, and tsked. "Oh, well!" She kissed Kim's cheek and patted Scott's face. "I'm so happy to see you! Such a nice couple!"

Scott winked. Kim shrugged. Rosalie would believe what she wanted. It was impossible to get it through the woman's head that Kim and Scott, two young, attractive, single people, could be anything but wildly in love.

"Your table is open tonight. Settle in and I'll get you some wine!" She bustled off without waiting for a reply.

Scott grinned, a dimple flashing in his left cheek. "She doesn't believe in platonic relationships between men and women, does she?"

"Maybe. Probably not." Kim shrugged again, spread her napkin in her lap. "It's more that she can't believe a nice girl like me isn't married yet. She's afraid I'll end up on the shelf."

He chuckled

Mama brought back red wine and poured generous measures into both glasses, in spite of the fact that Scott had protested on various occasions that he didn't drink. She would also not allow them to order, but said she'd bring the best of the evening.

"I love this place," he said, pushing his wineglass toward Kim. "But you've really gotta take me home with you someday."

"Oh, no," she said. "I'm sorry, but you think the marriage pressure is strong here? You haven't seen anything."

He lifted a shoulder. "I can handle it."

Kim shuddered. "You have no idea."

When he lowered his gaze, she realized—once again—that she'd been thoughtless. His mother had died a year or two before, which left him essentially orphaned.

Truth was, she knew he'd love her family—the whole, complicated lot of them—and they'd love him back. Her brothers, two older, one younger, would love his size and strength and manly good looks. Her sisters, both younger by quite a lot, would swoon in girlish crushes. Her father would grill him for financial stability, and her mother would feed him and be delighted at his enormous appetite.

"Maybe," Kim said. "You could bring a girl along."

He grinned. "I bet that could be arranged."

"No doubt."

When the salads came, Kim buttered hunks of bread and gave him one. "All right, partner mine," she said, raising her eyebrows, "do we want to talk about the caveman stuff while I was in Chicago, or are we going to forget it happened?"

Scott winced. "Sorry. Let's forget it."

"Are you sure? Because I don't want this to come up again at some future point and bite me in the butt. If you have an issue, let's get it out."

He was quiet for a minute, and watching him, Kim wondered why she never had been attracted to him romantically. He was drop-dead gorgeous, healthy, smart, sexy…everything. But she'd never thought of him like that at all.

As he seemed to mull over his answer, her heart sank. She'd never wanted him as a lover, but she hated to lose him as a partner. They worked extremely well together.

Finally, he lifted his head. "I did want you, at least sometimes I've wanted you. But I've always known you didn't think of me that way, and maybe it's just male ego wanting it to go the other way." His sideways grin was very, very cute. "I mean, jeez, Valenti, you're the only girl who *doesn't* like me."

She laughed. "Thank God I'm here for balance." She took a very, very tiny sip of wine. "All right, then, let's figure out what we've got with Mansour. Any more ideas about the next targets?"

"I'm thinking bridges. There were a couple of exchanges that made me just think we might need to look at trucks, transport, something like that."

Kim remembered the e-mail from Oracle before she left for Chicago. "Right. I had some intelligence that made me think the same thing. So where? What bridge or bridges?"

"Where are our candidates going to be over the next week?"

"We should check that. Also see about events, travel plans, maps, that kind of thing. There are huge crowds showing up in both camps, but the Secret

Service is there ahead of us in the venues, so that's less worrisome than it could be." She paused in the act of nearly biting into her bread. "I did collect a lot of information on the Columbus Day parades. It would be easier if people celebrated on either Sunday *or* Monday, but that's not the case."

"There are a couple of places that might be worth looking into more closely. Denver, for one," he said. "There's always a protest, which might lead to some chaos."

"Have we notified the Secret Service about all the possibilities?"

"I sent it all over this afternoon. Haven't heard back yet. Maybe you'll get something from your mysterious source."

"I don't have a mysterious source!"

"Yes, you do. How long do you think I can work with you without knowing that?"

"It's your imagination, Shepherd."

He gave a disbelieving roll of his shoulders. "Whatever."

Mama brought out two heavy ceramic plates with *sogliola alla mugnaia,* steaming hot and fragrant, served with Mama's trademark, hot fresh fettucini tossed with butter and herbs. The scent of basil arrowed through Kim's middle, making her stomach growl. "It's been a long time since lunch," she said, digging in.

For a minute, they focused respectfully on the

food. "You still need to bring me home, Valenti. I'd like to hang out with your family."

"Get a date, and we'll go on Sunday, how's that?"

"Perfect."

"Let's sleep on the bridges and things. Maybe something will bubble up."

They ate in companionable silence for a while, then Scott said, "I hear you got a promotion."

"Yeah. Go figure." She looked at him warily. "Are you mad?"

"When did I turn into some petty loser who takes offense at your accomplishments, Kim?" He scowled at her over his water glass. "Seriously. You've been very weird."

"Sorry. You're right." She poked her fork into the pasta. "I'm not sure what I'm thinking." But as had happened this morning, as she bent her head, she was assaulted with a vision of Lex, lean and long and dark, bending in to kiss her. She thought of him naked, standing in the kitchen aroused and hot. Her body flushed.

"You gotta stop thinking of that guy around me," Scott said. "You should see your face right now."

"Really?" She straightened, brushed hair away from her cheeks. "Sorry."

He shook his head, smiling slightly. "Don't be. It's good to see you fall."

Kim frowned. "I'm not *falling*."

"Whatever you say, Valenti."

Chapter 14

By the time she made it to the enclave of her condo that night, Kim was tired. Definitely not in the mood for the reporters she found, clustered like beetles around her apartment. With grim determination, she simply powered through them with one hand up, refusing to talk or answer the usual volley of questions.

She was also not in the mood for the message she had waiting from Marc. "You could have let me know," he said petulantly. "I didn't need to see you on the news with some guy. I mean, I know we don't have any claim, but, jeez, Kim, you were obviously hot for the guy."

Aloud, to the voice mail, she said, "You dope,"

and pressed the button to go on to the next message. It was from her mother. "Call me, Kim. You know me. I just need to know you're okay and home safely."

The last message was from Lex. "Hey, darlin'," he drawled, "we didn't officially exchange phone numbers, but I used my considerable influence to find your unlisted number. Give me a call." He left his number. Kim scrambled to find a piece of paper fast enough, then played the message again to be sure.

Hard to believe, looking around, that it had only been two nights away from home. That three nights ago, Marc had been here and she'd never met Lex Tanner.

At least in the flesh.

And what flesh it had turned out to be.

Frowning, she kicked off her shoes and took the bag upstairs to unpack. He was pretty dangerous to her peace of mind—and her *goals*—if everyone she met kept saying how smitten she obviously was. How to rein it in?

"Good question," she said to the mirror, leaning forward to examine the damage more closely. Her eye was going to have its worst day tomorrow, she figured, when the bruises turned green and yellow streaked with red. Of her facial injuries, it was by far the most gory looking—and it hurt the least. Her lip, now, which had been cut on the inside and only looked a little swollen—it hurt.

Her ear was hot, ugly and painful. Tenderly touching the edges, she vowed to make Ugly Face pay if she ever ran into him again. She'd had a lot of injuries in her time, but this ear thing was one of the worst. It seemed that everything jarred it.

She unpacked her bag, threw the dirty clothes in the laundry and headed down to the kitchen for some tea when the phone rang. Checking her caller ID to make sure it wasn't Marc, calling to check on her, Kim saw another name she recognized. Victoria Patton was a reporter for UBC and a fellow Athena student who had been a little bit ahead of Kim in school. Kim had admired the dark-haired, vivacious Tory from afar, but hadn't run in her circle.

She picked up the phone, intrigued. "Hello?"

"Hi, Kim. I'm sure you've had a million phone calls, but this is Tory Patton. We were at the Athena Academy together, though you might not remember me."

"Tory! Of course I remember you." Kim chuckled. "I had a terrible case of hero worship on you."

"Congratulations on your coup in Chicago. That was excellent work, and you made us all look terrific."

"Thanks. I had a lot of help."

"Right." Tory paused. "Kim, I'd really like to do a story on you. Is that possible?"

Kim had seen Tory's work—a reporter based in New York, she'd covered a number of huge stories over the years, not the least of which had been coverage last year of the only man to survive a hostage situation in the Central American country of Puerto Isla. The man had been a Navy SEAL, and his return to the U.S. had led to Tory breaking the truth to the country about President James Whitlow's campaign contributions from drug runners. "I'm honored, of course," Kim said, "but I hardly think I can give you the kind of story you're used to."

"You're modest, Kim. That's not a bad quality. But you're not seeing how dramatic and interesting this is."

"I don't want to talk about my brother, okay?"

"No problem. You have a right to your privacy."

"All right, then. How do you want to set this up?"

"I can fly in first thing tomorrow, if you like."

Kim frowned. "How long will it take?"

"An hour, maybe. I'll bring a cameraman, and we'll tape the whole interview and then cut and paste."

For a minute, Kim hesitated. "All right."

"You've done a lot of good, Kim. We're very proud of you."

Kim's ear suddenly ached, and she put two gentle fingers to it. "Thanks."

"All right. What time is good? Noon?"

"Sure. I'll see you then."

The phone had not been on the hook more than three seconds when it rang again. Checking caller ID, Kim saw it was a Chicago number and her heart jumped. She grabbed the phone, took a breath and said, "Hello?" in her best voice.

"Ms. Valenti?" said a woman's voice.

Damn. She was tempted to say, "Wrong number," but felt so idiotic about jumping for a phone call from a man that she just sighed with irritation. "Yes."

"My name is Lucinda Orange. I'm from the *Chicago Tribune*. I'd like to interview you for my column."

"Not tonight."

"All right. When would be good?"

"I don't know. Maybe never. I don't know why I'm this big celebrity today."

"You don't know." It wasn't a question, exactly, more like the droll recitation of an older sister. "Can I tell you?"

"Sure. Whatever."

"You're young, beautiful, tough, smart, and you looked like Angelina Jolie coming out of that ceiling. Every man in the audience had a hard-on—but that's not what I want to write about. I want to write about you for all the young women who are going to think you're fantastic."

Kim couldn't help it—she snorted in appreciation for the frank language. "All right, Ms.—what was your name?"

"Lucinda Orange."

"Ms. Orange, what kind of column do you write?"

"Commentary on women's lives and issues."

"And what's your angle?"

"You mean are you going to look good or bad in print?"

"Yeah."

"Good, Ms. Valenti." The woman laughed in a throaty, pleasant way. "I admire you. That I can promise you."

"All right. I'll give an interview, but I need to do it when I'm fresh. Call me tomorrow at ten, at this number." She gave her the office number.

When she hung up from the call, she picked it up immediately and called her mother. "Hey, Ma," she said.

"Kim! How are you, honey? You looked terrible on TV."

"Gee, thanks."

"You know what I mean. You were obviously injured, and you know that worries me. What happened?"

A thudding headache began at the base of Kim's neck. "You know, Mom, I'm really tired. I can't face another long catalog of the whole thing tonight, but I promise I'll let you look me over head to toe on Sunday, okay?"

"Fair enough. Are you going to bring that gorgeous creature you were with last night? Lex, is it?"

"Mom, he lives in Chicago."

"But he's Italian, isn't he? That would make your father so happy, and you have to admit, he's a very nice-looking man."

"Yeah, and he works for the bomb squad! Not great life odds there."

"Oh, please," her mother said dismissively. "No worse than a firefighter or a policeman or a sol—" She halted.

"Or a soldier," Kim said. "Exactly."

"Bomb squad is definitely better than combat soldiers."

Kim silently rolled her eyes. "Ma, enough. I'm tired. I am not bringing him to dinner on Sunday. I am, however, bringing my partner, Scott, because he's missing his family and he needs some love and attention. He is not husband material. Tell my father."

Eileen chuckled. "All right, baby. You go get some sleep and I'll see you on Sunday. Love you."

"Love you, too. Kiss my dad."

She hung up and rubbed her eyes. What day was it, anyway? When could she sleep in? It was Thursday. Not so bad. One more day.

The phone rang again. Kim groaned. Looking at caller ID, she saw it was—again—a Chicago number, but this time she picked up the number she'd written down for Lex and checked it. Bingo.

Her heart leaped, flipped, squeezed. Something. It hurt. "Don't do this, Kim," she said to herself. "Don't make him into something he's not, some beautiful perfect guy."

On the fourth ring, she picked it up. "Hello?"

"How you doin', darlin'?" said a rich, deep, Southern voice.

As if she were Pavlov's dog, Kim's tailbone went soft. "I'm all right, Lex. How are you?"

"Had better days. I can't stop thinking about you."

She fell on the couch, covered her forehead with an arm. And she did something she almost never did with a man—she let down her guard. A little bit. "I know what you mean."

"You thought about me?"

"Yes."

"What did you think about?"

"Oh, no, you don't. I'm not going to sit here and feed your ego, Mr. Tanner."

"If I feed yours first?"

She laughed, suddenly transported to last night, when his long fingers had been entwined with hers. "Well, if you like."

"I've been thinking about the way your shoulders look when you're tense and worried."

"Oh." Not what she'd expected.

"And when you were all worn out the night before last, one eyelid drooped more than the other."

"That's what you've been thinking about?"

"And you snore. You snored before you hardly hit that bed."

"How is this feeding my ego, exactly?"

"It's not," he said slowly. "But it's all true. I was thinking about those things."

"Don't get mushy on me, Tanner."

He laughed. The sound was low and wicked. "What do you want to hear, darlin'?"

"No, it's your turn. I was thinking about you, too. I was thinking about how—" Suddenly there were too many things in her head. The clarity of his eyes. The softness of his mouth. "You have a mouth just like Denzel Washington, you know that?"

"Is that right. Nobody every told me that before. He's such a big-time movie star, I guess that's good, right?"

"It's good."

"You like my mouth, then?"

"I do."

His voice dropped an octave. "You know what I've *really* been thinking about, sugar?"

"I bet I can guess."

"Your bare breasts when you had that gun in your hand. Hottest damned thing I ever saw in my life."

"Mmm. Thought you weren't looking?"

"You knew I was lying, even then."

"Yeah."

"When can I see you?"

"I thought you were going to be here next week for something."

"I don't want to wait that long. How about this weekend?"

Kim thought of his body, his vivid blue eyes—and

she also felt a slight sense of panic. Too fast. Too much. "No."

His laughter was the last thing she expected. "I'm hanging up now, Kim. Don't worry."

And he was gone.

Chapter 15

Friday, October 8

Before she went to work the next morning, Kim checked e-mail from Oracle and found a message waiting.

To: Ariadne@orcl.org
From: Delphi@orcl.org
Subject: Lead on-site planning
Several sources are pointing to the possibility of a plot to destroy a bridge with a truck bomb. Major speculation that the target is either Golden Gate or Brooklyn Bridge, but some leads point to

George Washington. Thanks to usual jealousy, some information has been withheld from certain agencies, which makes the connection to GW less obvious.

Security to all major bridges nationwide has been increased, but thanks to current policies designed to keep the public in a state of fear and off the current administration's involvement in Puerto Isla and Berzhaan, no one is taking the bridge threat seriously. Very important to discover which bridge is the target and take steps now to prevent it. Strong evidence suggests bombing slated for the upcoming Columbus Day weekend. Be advised— level four warning.

Possible helps: Valerie Kane at CIA, 202-555-9016; Karl Gibson at New York City Police, 212-555-3173. Both have files on Mansour and truck thievery.

Good luck.

Delphi

Kim had often wondered if Delphi had lost someone in the Puerto Isla debacle, when President Whitlow had sent in a SEAL force to rescue hostages who had turned out to be American drug runners. The SEALs had nearly all been killed, a massacre that should never have happened. The subject seemed to make Delphi particularly touchy.

One thing was clear: the Oracle group wanted Whitlow out of office. Now.

Kim made notes on the information, and stopped on the way in to work to buy a latte for herself and Scott. He was in the parking lot when she arrived, looking fresh and athletic in spite of the cold, gray day. She handed him his paper cup of nonfat, triple venti latte. "Jeez, Shepherd, you look like 'Rocky Mountain High' all by yourself."

He grinned, looking like his normal self. "Thanks. I found some things." He waved a sheaf of papers. "I think we're looking at an event within just a few days."

Kim nodded. "Me, too." She let him hold the door for her as she pulled out her ID. They passed through security and took an elevator to their floor and carried their briefcases into a small conference room. "I'm going to grab a couple of things from my desk," Kim said.

"Yeah, I'm gonna drop this coat, then check e-mail."

"Ten minutes, back here?"

"Right."

Kim flipped her monitor on, then hit the icon to collect e-mail. While she waited for it to download, she hung up her coat, shook down her sleeves, flipped through the in-box that had collected a surprising amount of material overnight. Most of it was fact-checking documentation, hard-copy printouts of various electronic communications. A co-worker had stuck in a newspaper cartoon showing President Whitlow as a Fidel-type politician smoking a cigar called Berzhaan.

There were several e-mails, all related to the intelligence gathered through the Q-group e-mails. Kim printed out the new e-mails collected from the cell overnight—seven of them, which was quite a lot for a twelve-hour period—and took them to the small conference room. Since they'd broken the code, the e-mails were intercepted, translated, then deciphered before Kim received them. She insisted upon receiving the originals, as well, not content to trust others with translation.

As she waited for Scott, she highlighted phrases that seemed important.

"Hey, gorgeous," said a voice from behind her.

The voice. Kim spun around, sure she wasn't hearing correctly.

But there he was. Lex, cleanly shaved, dressed in black slacks, black long-sleeved shirt, t.e.

He looked very, very good.

Kim stood up. Her hands felt awkward, so she tried to put them in the back pockets of her jeans, but she was wearing a skirt. "Lex! What are you doing here?"

"Been assigned to help."

"Us?"

"This case. They're thinking it's a whole lot of explosives. Fourteen moving vans have been stolen in the past three weeks."

"Moving vans." Kim blinked, trying to imagine what a moving van full of explosives could do to a bridge.

From behind him, Scott hustled in, carrying a box of files. "Hey," he said, lifting his chin toward Lex. "You the new guy? Oh—hey. You're the FBI guy."

Next to Scott's hale outdoorsy look, Lex looked ethnic and lean, a coyote next to a big fluffy St. Bernard. "Lex Tanner," he said, extending a hand. "You must be Scott."

"Good to meet you."

Kim let go of a breath she didn't know she was holding. "Let's see what we've got." She sat down and pulled out her notes. "We've got moving vans. Bridges. Mansour is still on the loose, with pretty serious financial backing."

"Have we figured out who is bankrolling this guy anyway?"

"Not yet. He's anti-CIA and -U.S.A. and anti-Kemini, so I'd put my money on the usual suspects. Islamic extremists, disgruntled rich Berzhaanians who want the Keminis squashed."

Lex scowled. "But the Chicago cell seems to be richer than usual. The kind of money which usually only comes from two kinds of vice, either drugs or arms deals."

Kim thought of the nonnative Arabic speaker at

the television station. "There was definitely a non-Arab at the station. He's one of the guys that got away with Mansour. The station manager was also involved somehow, so there's an American connection."

Scott swore.

"Where there's money to be made," Kim said with a shrug, "there's bound to be people wanting to make it. It's something we can research a little more." She shifted gears. "Scott, did you decide which of the e-mail-loop guys might be Mansour? Maybe we can figure out some clues to his whereabouts from that."

"You might want to take a look. You're better at some of the subtle stuff." He pulled out a yellow tablet with scribbles on it. "I do have some ideas on the bridge that might be targeted, however. The three that seem to generate the most interest from terrorist types are the famous ones—" he ticked them off on his fingers "—Golden Gate, Brooklyn and George Washington."

Kim nodded, pleased that she wasn't the one to bring up the George Washington Bridge.

"I also looked up whatever major bridges might be targeted in the heartland—over the Missouri and Mississippi, any bridges along Interstate Highways, any arteries into military bases, that kind of thing. A couple important ones came up—the I-40 Mississippi River Bridge in Memphis; the Houston Ship Channel Bridge, the Seattle I-90 to Mercer Island."

He pulled out pictures of the bridges, spread them in a row across the top of the table. "This is where you come in, Tanner, and why I requested you. How do you blow up a bridge? Which of these bridges is a good target and which ones aren't worth the trouble?"

Lex stood up, poked one of the pictures. "The Memphis bridge is a beauty," he drawled. "But she's built to withstand a level 7 earthquake, so she'd be hard to bring down completely."

"Earthquakes in Memphis?" Kim said.

"One of the most dangerous fault lines in the country is right through that Mississippi farmland." He lifted a shoulder. "It's not as unstable as the San Andreas, but it's serious."

"Does that kick out the Golden Gate, too, then?" Scott asked.

"I wouldn't rule it out, just because it's so symbolic, so visible, but she'd probably hold up—she's been retrofitted to withstand an 8.3," Lex said.

"How do you *know* this stuff?" Kim asked.

"This isn't the first time terrorists have made noises about American bridges. I've made it my business to find out what I can," Lex said. "There are ways to bring almost anything down if you have enough explosives—but some bridges are more interesting than others."

"Right." Kim frowned. "Terrorists want the most bang for the buck, right? So, the busiest bridges?

The ones that would disrupt commerce most severely?"

Scott said, "But think about 9/11. It was a hit designed to take out a lot of people, but also to strike at the country's ideology."

"True."

"So—it's Columbus Day weekend, right? Maybe they'll hit parades or parades going over bridges, something like that."

"By that reasoning, then I like the George Washington bridge," Kim said.

"Hmm." Lex nodded agreement. "That's a possibility. It also has a double tier structure, which would make it easier to do real damage—the vehicles on the lower level blow, which blows upward, then the weight comes down and knocks things loose in a downward motion."

"And it's New York again," Kim added. "The double whammy."

"Right." Scott frowned. "That's just a guess—we don't want to put all our eggs in one basket, just in case it isn't right."

"No, I think it might be the George Washington bridge. Just a gut feeling," Kim said.

Scott said, "Oh, yeah? Your secret source backs me up, huh?"

Kim shook her head and rolled her eyes. "Keep telling you…"

"Secret source?" Lex asked, perking up.

"He's full of it," Kim said.

"Nah, Lex. She has like a secret identity, and there's some big secret society."

"Is that right?" Lex watched her a little too closely.

Kim grabbed a stack of papers. "I guess my secret is out—I'm really the Green Flashlight, cousin to the Green Lantern. In my off-hours, I wear a skin-tight—"

"Ooh, I like that idea."

"—gown with green shoes, and it gives me special powers so I can go out and bring back Truth, Justice and the American Way." She rolled her eyes. "Please." Glancing at the clock, she saw that it was nearly noon. Tory would be arriving soon and Kim wanted to look her best. "Now, if you'll excuse me, gentlemen, I've got a media interview to take."

Scott chuckled. "I'll make the phone calls to the CIA this time, huh?"

"With my blessing," Kim said. "Can you imagine what he'll be like now that I was right again?"

"Maybe he'll lighten up."

"Right. Lex, of course you can take the FBI. I'll call the guy on the NYPD."

"What guy?" Scott asked.

"The old policeman, the one in New York City." Too late, Kim realized she'd taken that information from Oracle. Heat threatened to spill into her face, and she could not give herself away like that. Covering as fast as she could, she shook her head. "It must not have been you I discussed this with. Maybe it was Diana. Last night on the phone."

Lex and Scott both sat at the table and just looked at her, the Snow White and Rose Red of big tough guys, one so blond and sturdy and outdoorsy Colorado, the other dark and lean and severe. "No secret society, huh?" Lex said.

"No secret code?" Scott added.

"Don't be ridiculous." She grabbed her papers and took off. "See you guys later."

Chapter 16

Kim first dialed the policeman in New York City, Karl Gibson. She asked for him, gave her name and was put through immediately. He picked up. "Gibson."

She introduced herself and explained the situation. "I'm looking for any clues, any ideas, any information that might help us piece together where these guys are gonna strike next."

"All right. What can I tell you?"

Kim was not entirely certain why Oracle had told her to call the policeman, so she winged it. "Have you arrested or had contact with any Berzhaan rebels or Keminis or anything related to them in the past few weeks?"

"We did," he said. "We had a tip that there was a

group centered around a tire shop near the George Washington bridge. We paid 'em a visit and found a whole lot of explosives."

"Really. A tire center?"

"Yeah. Let's see if I can get you the name."

Kim waited, pencil poised above her paper. He said, "Here it is—Hafiz abu Malik Abd-Human."

"Very good. So did you arrest a group there?"

"We got a couple of guys," he said, "but they're peons and they're not about to talk."

"You didn't get the owner?"

"No. He was out of town. We recovered a shitload of explosives though, I'll tell you that. Most of them were packed into a single moving van. Could have taken out a sizable building."

"Or a bridge?"

"Oh, yeah. No problem."

"All right, thank you. I'll keep you posted on anything that seems to feed into it."

She hung up and frowned. Who else had talked about tires? She flipped through her notes, through the paragraphs sent via Oracle. Nothing.

She knew it was somewhere. She just had to remember.

A small electronic noise alerted her to incoming e-mail. Kim switched screens and found a note from Scott.

Check this out.

He included links to articles on earthquake pre-
paredness, bridge stability and a lengthy article on
the Coronado bridge.

I'm thinking we need to look more into this one.

Kim wrote back:

Maybe. Let me do some more translations.

She picked up the file of original, decoded docu-
ments, which were all in Arabic, and began to sort
through them, dividing them into stacks according
to who wrote them.

Her phone rang. "Agent Valenti," said the receptionist, "there's a camera crew here to see you."

"Sure." Kim brushed hair from her face, wondering just how bad she'd look on camera. She glanced
around at the room, and realized this part could be embarrassing. "Put the woman on the phone, will you?"

The phone changed hands. "Tory," Kim said.
"Let's try to keep this as low-key as possible, all
right? I don't want a lot of resentment between me
and the rest of the staff."

"You want to meet us down here instead of up
there? I'd be happy to do that."

For a minute, she was very tempted, then she

thought of Scott and Lex, and the need to include them in the interview. "No, that's all right. We'll meet you in the conference room."

She popped her head in Scott's office. Both Lex and Scott were bent over something spread out on the desk. "C'mon, gang," she said. "It's showtime. The UBC crew is here."

"What are you talking about?" Scott said with annoyance.

"Television. They want to do a story, and this woman is a graduate of the Athena Academy, too, so I know she'll do a good job. C'mon. Let's just get it done and get back to work."

Scott took a comb out of his pocket. "Is she cute?"

"Very."

"Excellent." He smoothed his hair.

Lex was grinning at Kim. "What?" she asked.

"You're gonna look real cute."

"Don't be sarcastic. There's nothing I can do."

He sidled up to her. "You look hot to me, honey."

"Sigh," Kim said. "Let's go."

Just as they came into the hallway, Tory and her cameraman came from the elevator. Kim had seen Tory at Athena as a teen and on television many times, but it was still startling to see her tiny, neat beauty in person as an adult. Dressed in a white suit with a red blouse, Tory looked as crisp as a new dollar bill. "Kim!" she said warmly, coming forward to hold out her hand. "I'd say you look wonderful, but you'd know it was a lie."

Kim chuckled. "I'm not a big makeup kind of girl. Do you want to do something about the face?"

Tory firmly shook her head. "Not at all. You're fine." She turned and introduced her cameraman. "This is Jay."

"Nice to meet you," Kim said, shaking her hand.

"That was really something, you at the television station," he said with a flirtatious smile.

Kim thought of what the columnist told her—that she was a male fantasy. "Thanks. Let's go to the conference room, shall we? My partner is there, along with Lex Tanner, who was critical in defusing the bomb at the airport."

"Excellent," Tory said. "And don't mind Jay, he flirts with all the hot women."

Jay laughed and followed them into the room. Kim introduced everyone, watching as Scott straightened, ready to charm his way into the tiny brunette's long-term memory. Jay had competition in the flirting department. "Cool it, Shepherd," she said in his ear. "I think she's involved with someone pretty seriously." She'd heard rumors that Tory was dating Bennington Forsythe, the playboy brother of another Athena grad, Alexandra.

The cameraman checked light levels and set them all up around the conference table. Tory said, "I'm mainly focusing on Kim if you don't mind, guys. I'll do a clip with each of you, but it makes a better story if she's the main hook."

"But they were instrumental!" Kim protested.

"Fine with me," Lex said.

"She did the work," Scott added. "Do you want us to clear out then?"

"Up to you."

"Let's go," Lex said, and they left.

Kim gnawed her lip for a minute. "I didn't do it on my own," she said. "I've had tons of help."

Tory clipped a mike to Kim's blouse. "I know. I also know you've distinguished yourself." She grinned. "Love that video of you coming out of the ceiling."

Kim chuckled. "Seems to be a favorite moment."

"Let's get started."

Putting a hand to her tummy, Kim said, "I'm nervous, I think."

"All right. We'll just start the cameras and shoot some footage, and we can talk about Athena Academy to start with. Just talk, just as we've been doing. How's that?"

"Okay."

Tory gave Ben the signal, and the camera started rolling. "Tell me, Kim," she said, "what was it like for you to leave home and go to the Athena Academy?"

"I was very excited," Kim said. "But also terrified. It was a very long way from home, and I'd never been away from my very large family. But I was also very excited at the things we were studying—languages and math and all the physical activities. Girls were not really encouraged to be very, very physical in my neighborhood, and I loved that part of Athena."

Tory smiled, and Kim realized her nervousness was gone. "Good," Tory said. "Let's talk about the Chicago bomb."

Kim nodded. The interview covered much the same ground as the questions that had been asked and answered till now, though Tory gave it a better, more sophisticated spin.

When it was over, Kim shook her hand again. "That was relatively painless."

"Good. I'll give you a call when it's going to air. I think we have some good material."

"Thanks."

"I'll go film a little with the boys, then, and talk to you soon."

Four hours later, Kim was twittery and jumpy as the clock crept closer and closer to 5:00 p.m. and the time they would quit and then Lex would—what? Go stay in a hotel nearby? Try to go out with her? Come to her apartment? She didn't know.

As she sorted through code and e-mails in the original Arabic, trying to piece together some usable picture of what the terrorist cell had planned, her mind circled around and around and around the fact of Lex. Lex and the fact that he was in town. And she didn't know what was going on tonight.

That was the trouble. No, the *fact* of him was the trouble. A man who wasn't going to ever take no for an answer, who was so alluring and intriguing and different from anyone she'd ever met that she was—for the first time in her life—in danger of actually falling in love.

And he knew it. How did he know? Was he so used to seducing women of all ilks that he just knew which buttons to push? Was she falling for a very sincere player?

And wasn't *sincere player* an oxymoron?

"Oh, good grief, Valenti," she muttered to herself in exasperation at about three in the afternoon. She pushed away from her desk and marched to the ladies' room, refusing to even glance toward the room where Lex was working with Scott on bridge schematics.

In the bathroom, she turned the tap on cold and put her hands under it, rinsing them over and over as she lectured herself. This was exactly what she did not want to do: work herself up into a lather over a man. Start letting him take over her thoughts. Invade her work time. Claim her life, inch by inch.

Kim glared at herself in the mirror. "Stop it," she said aloud.

But she examined her lips closely, wishing they

were more shapely. Her mother had a beautiful, perfect mouth. Why hadn't she gotten it? Certainly she wished the black eye wasn't so bad. It looked awful today. She smoothed her skirt, backed up and looked at her butt in the mirror. Definitely not little.

She realized what she was doing and halted.

Insane. She was insane. Maybe the only answer was just to sleep with him and get him out of her system. Then she could go back to Marc and her ambitions and stop mooning.

"Get a grip. He's only a guy."

But she was still tense three hours later when she closed the door to her condo and automatically clicked the alarm system on. Before she moved farther into the apartment, she kicked off her shoes, then holding the mail in one hand, she padded into the room, shedding keys, coat, purse. It was good to be home, in the silence of her sanctuary, where there was no lure of Lex, no hammering awareness dragging on her all day.

God, he had the pheromones of a rock star.

Standing beside the trash can, she sorted through the mail, tossing circulars and flyers from mortgage lenders into the trash, sliding the credit card and cell phone bills into a folder on the small table by the kitchen window.

It was then that she spied the wire. A blue wire running along her windowsill.

A wash of foreboding poured down her spine. Dropping the mail on the table and without touching it, she followed the thin blue wire to see where it would go.

It snaked down the wall, along the floor, to the window in her study, then along the floor again, out of the study, up the wall toward the loft bedroom. Kim felt sweat start to prickle beneath her blouse. Grimly, she raced up the stairs and found what she knew she would: the bedroom windows were wired, too.

And the front door. And the back door, and every window in the condo.

The bomb was barely out of sight—simply sitting on the floor behind the small table next to her front door—wired into her home security system. She'd armed it herself when she came in. They'd wanted her to know she was trapped.

Kim swore.

She was about to pick up the telephone when she realized that the burglar alarm was wired into the phone. Could a ring set it off? She grabbed the phone and turned it over. For a long moment she stared at the line that connected it to the wall, wondering if it, too, was booby-trapped. If she just turned off the ringer, maybe that would be safer. Her upper lip was sweating. She clicked the switch to the off position.

From behind her came a shrill, electronic ring. Kim startled so hard she nearly dropped the phone, and her biological reaction was a jolt to the heart so fierce it felt as though someone jammed a lance through it.

Her cell phone. Ringing in her purse. Kim grabbed it, saw by caller ID that it was the office calling. "Hello?" she barked.

"Kim, thank God," Lex said. "Did I catch you before you got home?"

"No, unfortunately." She took a breath. "If I unplug the phone line, will it arm the bomb attached to my security system?"

"Fuck."

"My sentiments exactly."

"Turn off the ringer on your phone immediately. And can you see your front walk? Nobody should ring the doorbell."

"I don't know if I can disconnect the doorbell."

"No! Don't." He cleared his throat. "I'm going to walk you through disarming it. Don't worry."

She chuckled bitterly. "I'll do my best."

"Walk me through it. Tell me everything you can see."

Kim told him about the windows and doors, the thin blue wire trussing her into her house like a doomed turkey. Told him about the wires trailing up the wall to her security system. "And the wires go into a white boxlike package, very neat, sitting beside the wall, near the front door."

There was a little pause from his end. "Okay. This

is a little different scenario than the bomb we had at the airport."

"I get that."

"It's hard to know if this is wired to time or to movement. Don't touch it, but tell me what you see about where the lines go into the box. Usually, the initiator is close to the top."

"There's nothing, really," Kim said. "Just a smooth box."

"Hold on a second." He covered the receiver and Kim could hear the garbled sound of conversation—Lex asking a question, getting an answer, asking another question.

He came back on the line. "Tell me the layout of your apartment."

"Front door opens into a living room that's a good size. Stairs go up to my bedroom, which has an open loft that overlooks the living room. There's a bathroom upstairs." She took a breath, eyed the bomb. It looked so innocuous. "Back downstairs, you go into the kitchen, and there's a second bedroom-study off the kitchen."

"How much of a wall between the living room and the back study?"

Kim lifted a shoulder, her spirits sinking as she guessed what he was going to have her do. "Pretty serious walls, actually. The main crossbeam, then two smaller walls. The study is also in a little area that juts out from the rest of the apartment, so it's just a single-level roof."

"Okay. Let me think a second here."

Kim waited. Her arms ached with tension. With the need to act. She didn't want to blow up her condo. She liked it. There had to be a better way. "Lex—"

"I want you to prepare an area in the back room as if there was a tornado. Couch cushions, pillows, that kind of thing, all right?"

"Lex, I don't want to blow up the apartment. It's my home."

"I can appreciate that, Valenti. But you have no idea what this bomb could do, and I'm not taking chances. Insurance will repair the condo."

"But—"

"Get the pillows." It wasn't a request.

She put down the phone and followed orders, carrying cushions and pillows into the back room. Then, before she picked up the phone, she took down paintings, and gathered all the knickknacks from her Arizona youth, and put them under the desk in the study.

"Done," she said, picking up the phone. "Now what?"

"You say the whole house is wired, every window?"

"Yeah." Outside, there was a commotion, and Kim looked out to the parking lot to see police cars, fire trucks and all her neighbors being herded away from the area.

Kim felt faintly ill and looked down at the bomb. How had Lex known there was a problem here, anyway? "Can't you send one of those bomb squad guys in here?"

"If you open the door, the bomb blows. Sorry."

She swallowed. "This is scaring the shit out of me, Luthor."

"I want it to. Fear will make you careful."

"Let's get it over with."

"You see the scenario here—the bomber was pretty sure you'd go out the front door, so that's where the device is located, but it's keyed into the security system, so it will blow if the perimeter is disturbed."

"Right."

"Go to your study, get into position as well as you can—cover your head, all that—then open the window with a long handle. Maybe a broom? Then dive under your desk."

"I don't know if I can open these windows with a broom. They're aluminum, with a pretty tight fit and no lip to speak of."

"What happens with your alarm if you break a window? Does the alarm go off or do you have to move the window physically?"

"I would guess it goes off if the window breaks. I haven't tried it."

"Work with me, Kim, dammit. It's not funny."

"I'm not trying to be funny. I don't know the an-

swer to your question! That was honest." She rubbed
a spot on her chest, realizing that her heart was rushing, speeding, tumbling over itself. "Is this going to
kill me?"

"No. Not if you don't take chances."

"No, I'm not going to die because I need to collect on a debt you owe me," she said, and headed into
the study.

"Is that right?"

"Yeah." In the study, she shoved her second desk
against the far wall, and put a cushion beneath it. She
banged her hip, hard, and swore. "I'm in the study,
everything is ready. I can try breaking the window
with a..." She looked around, picked up a hefty can-
dleholder made of iron. "An iron candlestick."

"Can you throw it? You can't be standing up and
swinging it. It's gotta have heft enough that you can
do it from beneath the desk."

"No, I can throw it." A ripple of anticipation or
terror or both went through her as she imagined the
explosion. "Now what?"

"Get a broomstick, too, something long enough
that you can use it to shove open the window if
breaking the window doesn't work."

She dashed into the kitchen, grabbed the broom,
dashed back in. "Can we get this over with now?"

"Yep. Get in position beneath the desk. Cover
your head, throw the candlestick and put your knees
up, tuck your head down with your hands—"

"Yeah, yeah, yeah," Kim said. "Tornado position. I got it."

"Keep the phone on, will ya?"

"Sure. Are you ready?"

There was a pause. "I hate this."

"Not half as much as I do."

"You're gonna be fine, Valenti. Get ready. Tell me just before you're going to throw the candlestick."

Kim tucked herself beneath the desk, settled her cushions around her properly, with a sofa pillow on her shoulders, the phone in one hand. Her heart was racing.

"Okay, Lex, I'm putting down the phone now. I'll count to three as loud as I can so you know when I'm throwing it. Then…uh…I hope I'll be talking to you in a minute."

"Got it."

Kim braced one more cushion in place, then picked up the candlestick, and counted aloud. "One! Two! Three!" She threw the candlestick in a hard arc, ducked backward and pulled the pillow over her head.

The bomb exploded.

Chapter 17

The explosion was louder than anything she'd ever heard. The sound was physical, carried in shock waves through her condo, slamming into walls, ceilings, rooms, reverberating at a decibel that threatened to shatter her eardrums. And it wasn't fast, as she'd expected, but seemed to vibrate through her head, arms, chest, teeth, a sound sucking everything else out of the world, for a very long time. A sense of pressure squeezed her body, all of it, and something slammed down overhead with a hard crack. The desk buckled over her, slamming into the sofa cushion over her head and shoulders, shoving her into an even tighter ball. Her head and face squeezed into a pillow, and for a second she couldn't breathe, couldn't move, and she thought with panic that it would be so ironic if she escaped being crashed or blown to bits but then was smothered in a pillow.

Don't panic.

Deal with the facts.

Can't breathe.

Why?

Pillow.

Move it.

Can't get my head turned.

Use your hands.

Arms are trapped, too tight.

Move your knees a little.

She tried pushing her knees down and the pillow shifted infinitesimally, enough that she could wiggle her head to the side, and slide her nose and mouth into a breathing hole in the dark, tight spot, and gulp in some dusty air.

"Lex?" she cried as loud as she could. "Can you hear me?"

The tinny sound of the phone came through the darkness, but she couldn't really hear it. With fierce effort, she tried to move her right arm against whatever was trapping it. She'd put the phone down right beside her knee—surely she could move that far.

But although she could move her fingers, the arm was smashed hard against her side. "Lex, I can't make out your words, but I'm safe. Stuck, but safe."

It couldn't have been more than a minute or two before she heard noises beyond her tight dark world. A dog barked distantly, and she heard a shout, then others farther away. A siren howled.

"Here!" she cried. "I'm in here!"

She realized in the dense darkness that her ear was really hurting again. Damn it. Her knee was getting a cramp.

Shouldn't she be able to see some cracks of light somewhere? Was it only that the pillows and cushions were blotting everything out, or was the darkness a sign of something more ominous? She thought of earthquake victims, buried in rubble for days.

Breathe.

Not that she was afraid of that happening now. The whole of the NSA knew exactly where she was. The complex had been surrounded by police and rescue personnel before the bomb even blew. She would not be here longer than ten minutes, a half hour at the outside.

Still, it was sobering to imagine.

Something dripped on her shoulder. Water? Where was water coming from? Oh, probably fire hoses. There was probably fire from the explosion. Of course they would have to put it out.

A sense of tightness grew in her chest and she focused on taking a long, slow deep breath, letting it out very slowly and easily. Stay calm. There was plenty of oxygen. She was not buried under tons of rubble. It was just the desk and maybe some house debris. She was not, as far as she could tell, injured.

A sound came from the phone, a tinny faraway sound. "I'm okay!" she tried to cry out, but it came out as a croak. Her throat was dry. "I'm okay!" she tried again.

Now her knee was really cramping and she tried to ease her position a little, pushing it to one side, moving her shoulders, trying to see how much movement she could get. Very little. She was in a more or less fetal position, with her knees bent, her arms gripping the cushion, her face sandwiched between the cushion she'd placed on her shoulders and the one in her chest. By easing the knee to the left slowly, she managed to get a little more space for breathing. A centimeter at a time, she eased her head to the right, pushing as hard as she could toward the faintly less-dead air space. She opened her eyes as wide as she could, and there was still no light.

A dog barked more urgently, and she heard an identifiable voice that didn't seem faraway. Maybe they'd made it to the back room finally. "Here!" she cried.

"We know you're there, Kim," a man's voice said. It seemed very close. "Can you hear me?"

"Yes! I'm fine."

"Good. Don't do a lot of moving, all right? There's a logistical problem with a roof beam and we're trying to get you out, but everything is pretty delicate. We don't want to get too much movement until I tell you to, okay?"

"Okay."

"It might take a little while, but you're safe. Trust me."

"I'm okay."

"Good. Hang in there!"

The sense of panic rose again. A roof beam. Don't move.

Breathe, she told herself. *Just breathe through it. Don't panic.*

It was hard to say how long she stayed crouched there. There was comfort in hearing the voices of the men on the other side of her darkness. Hearing the scrape and rattle and shouted directions, some of which she could make out and some she could not. There was discomfort in the tightness of her position, and an annoying drip of water coming through some crack she couldn't identify, and the pain in her injured ear.

And it was very difficult not to panic when she could not move a muscle. She didn't like closed places. Never had. Everyone had their difficulties, their weak spots. This was hers.

It was like a coffin. The most horrifying thing she could imagine was being buried alive. She hated the stories of people who'd been buried by mistake, not dead—

Stop.

—and they died there, the wood of the coffin scraped raw by fingers that could do no good.

Breathe.

She forced herself to bring her attention back to her breath. In. Out. She was not dying. She was not buried alive. There were people right on the other side of the wooden desk who knew she was there and were working to get her out.

Breathe. In. Out.

In the darkness, she thought of her brother Jason. It seemed she could almost smell him. Was he afraid at the end? Was he in some awful little prison cell before they decided to kill him, knowing what his end would be, or had they just grabbed him out of his truck and killed him?

"Don't get all dramatic, Sissie," Jason said in her ear. She felt his hand on her back, right between her shoulder blades. "It's all good. It's all good."

"We're in!" said a voice—a real voice—outside her enclave. "Kim, can you hear me?"

"Yes. Yes!"

"We've got to get a winch over here—there's a beam sitting right on the desk and we've got to drag it off. All right?"

She wanted to scream. She didn't. She swallowed hard and said, "Okay." Better than being dead. Better than being a hostage. Better than being an earthquake victim, buried beneath a thousand tons of debris in South America or Indonesia.

The oddly warm sense of a protective hand between her shoulder blades came back. "That's it, honey," said her brother's voice. "You're doing fine. Think of good things. Think of that day we found the frog palace at the pond behind Muller's store."

"Good idea," she said aloud. She called up the day—bright gold and green; summertime, leaves making dappled shadows on the grassy ground behind a small grocery. It was a waste area in the midst of the city, filled with trees and junk and the secret pond. Teenagers went there at night to have sex, and children chased tadpoles in the daytime. That afternoon, it was only she and Jason, humidity and heat enveloping them like a suit of armor. The frog palace was sitting at the end of the pond, beneath the trees—a little building some eccentric had built, with open rooms and puddles of water through it, and pagoda-style towers and roofs. It was freshly painted, the tips bright red.

"I thought of the frog palace whenever things got hard," he said, and his hand moved, easy and smooth, on her back. "Love ya, Sissie."

With the comfort of that hand, she drifted. It wasn't sleep, exactly, but it was a place of softness and no fear, a release of all things dark and sorrowful. It could have been moments or hours when she heard a new voice.

"Kim. Kim! Kim, can you hear me?"

"Lex?" she croaked. Then again, louder. "Lex?"

"I'm here. We're going to pull the beam off now. You should be outta there in a hot second, darlin'."

"Thank God," she said, but wasn't sure if he could hear her. Her throat felt raw. Dry.

There was a sound of engines, and a groaning. Shouts. And suddenly, the pressure over Kim's body eased. She couldn't see any lights, but she could suddenly breathe.

And move. She straightened, and kicked the pillow by her leg, and a sharp light blasted into her little cave. She winced, put a hand up to block it, but she didn't wait for anyone to pull her out, she fell forward into the air, sucking in a huge lungful, grateful to move her limbs.

Pinpricks of pain rushed through her arms and legs, her feet and hands, as the feeling came back. She tried to stand up, stumbled as her legs refused to hold her, and then there were hard, strong arms around her. "Hold on there, honey," Lex said. "I got you."

She leaned on him, grateful for the solidity, and gritted her teeth "I am so claustrophobic," she whispered. "Excuse me." She stumbled away, and threw up. It was impossible to say what she threw up on, since there was nothing recognizable around her.

Lex stood beside her. "I think we need to get you to the hospital and get you checked out."

Kim scowled at him "Don't be ridiculous." She pressed the back of her hand to her mouth. "I'm nauseated because I'm so relieved to get out, but I feel fine."

He smiled, his hands on his hips, and nodded in a funny way. "I appreciate that, Valenti, but you're at least gonna need a couple of stitches. You've got a few cuts, you know, just here and there."

"Do I?" She touched her face. Felt the smear of blood. "I had a pillow on my head."

His nostrils flared. "Good thing." He held out his arm, as if he were coaxing a small child. "Come on. Let's get you to the hospital. There's an ambulance over there."

Kim felt dizzy, and put her hand on his arm. "Okay. I guess that would be good."

He made a soft noise and gently cradled her head, kissed her temple. There was fierceness in the gesture, restraint in his strong palm and fingers. "God," he whispered.

For one minute, she just let herself rest there, leaning on the hard rectangle of his forearms, his hand on her head, his breath warm on her face. Finally she said, "I have a headache. Do you have any ibuprofen?"

He made a noise between exasperation and a laugh. "Here's your ride, honey," he said, and helped her into the ambulance.

Chapter 18

When Kim finally emerged from the emergency room, where she'd been x-rayed and stitched and washed up, Lex was sitting in the waiting room. He was slumped against the wall, his head back, his eyes closed. A magazine was open on his lap.

Kim halted for a moment, stung by the coyote beauty of his lean face, the high cheekbones and strong nose. He probably had been a very gawky teenager. The thought made her feel tender.

"Hey," she said, touching his knee.

He startled awake. "Oh! Hey!"

She smiled gently. "We gotta stop meeting like this, Luthor."

He peered at her with concern. "How are you?"

"No great damages. A few stitches." The ear—which had been torn open again, along with a six-inch gash along the top of her scalp from a sword of metal that had just missed her temple—was definitely sore. She had a headache still, but they'd given her some drugs to take before she went to bed. "Nothing broken. No concussion."

"Good." He stood. "Are you hungry?"

"Starving. I haven't had a meal since—" she frowned, thinking back "—a tuna sandwich at lunch."

"Can you hold on for about a half hour?"

"Sure, what's up?"

He raised his brows, took her hand. "The reason I knew there might be a bomb at your house is because—"

"They got Scott." Her stomach dropped. "Is he dead?"

"No. He's in critical condition, in intensive care. I thought you'd want to see him."

"Yeah."

In silence, they rode up in an elevator. Lex reached for her hand, but Kim couldn't bear it. Slid her hand out of his grasp.

"It's not you," she said.

"It's okay."

The hallway they entered was deeply hushed. Somewhere, someone wept quietly, and Kim could hear the soft beeping and breathing of machines. A guard sat outside Scott's room, a paperback novel in his hands. Lex flashed his badge. "This is his partner."

"Only one of you can go in at a time."

Kim opened the door. A nurse in a pale blue scrub suit was recording vitals on a clipboard. She looked up as Kim entered, and gave her a grave smile. "He's resting right now." she said very quietly. "He won't know you're here."

"I'll know," she said, and moved to the bed.

Scott was nearly unrecognizable. His face was black-and-blue and swollen, with cuts and scratches and stitches. One hand was bandaged in a way that made the bile rise in her throat. "Did he lose his hand?"

The nurse glanced toward the door. "You look like you were with him when it happened."

"Not exactly. Two different bombs."

The nurse had kind blue eyes and sturdy shoulders. "He lost the hand."

"What else?"

"Skull fracture. broken ribs, crushed pelvis." She paused. "Internal injuries."

"Such as?"

"Lacerated liver, lost spleen... we had to induce a coma to keep his brain from swelling too much."

Kim asked, "Is he going to live?"

"It's a good sign that he's made it this long," the nurse said levelly.

"Thank you."

The nurse hung the chart at the foot of his bed. On the way out, she squeezed Kim's arm, just above the elbow. "Don't stay long."

When she'd left, Kim bent over him and pressed her lips to his battered face. "I'm here, Scott," she said. "I'm so sorry. I thought I was doing the right thing, giving credit where credit was due."

The monitors blipped steadily. Heart rate, respiration, blood pressure. Something dripping from an IV attached to his arm. The stump of his arm lay against the white blanket, somehow obscene.

"You better not die. I'll be back here in the morning to read to you. We'll get these bastards, Scott, I swear it."

Behind her, Lex said, "C'mon. Let's go get some sloppy fast food and get you off your feet."

Kim squeezed Scott's hand, and let herself be led away.

Instead of fast food, however, they went to a hotel, where their floor was heavily guarded. "Orders," Lex said. "We can get room service."

"We're not in the same room, are we? Do you know what that would do to my reputation?"

"Not the same room." His nostrils flared as he pushed open his door, and pointed. "But I made sure they were adjoining."

"You don't expect sex, I hope."

"Not even." He opened his side of the door, and gave her the card key to her room. 'Go round and open that."

When Kim went to her room and opened the connecting door from her side, he said, "I won't sleep if I don't know you're safe." And very gently, he touched her face. "Are you all right?"

Kim ducked her chin. "Fine. I keep telling you I'm fine, except that I'm starving and I want a shower to wash off all the crud."

"Let's order and then you can have a shower"

"Did anyone think to get me some clothes to change into?"

Lex grinned, and pointed to a suitcase placed before the dresser. "One of the female officers went shopping for you."

She shrugged out of her coat, flung it on the bed. "Is my condo completely destroyed?"

He hesitated. Then nodded. "'Fraid so."

"At least I'm not dead."

"What do you want to eat, darlin'?" He picked up the phone. "Cheeseburger? Fries? Pizza?"

"Food. I just want some food. With meat. Fat. Cheeseburger is probably excellent." She was practically swaying where she sat, and made herself stand up and open the suitcase. As Lex asked for room service and started ordering food, she picked out a simple turquoise T-shirt and some sweats. No bras,

but there were panties in several small sizes. Bless
her, whoever she was. Good job.

The shower helped. As the dirt and sweat and
stickiness washed away, she could let the day go, too.
In the shower she could cry a little, let flow the tears
for Scott and the trauma of being trapped and the loss
of her home. She could do it privately in the shower,
where no one would feel compelled to make her feel
better or tell her it was okay.

It *wasn't* okay.

When she emerged she didn't bother to wipe the
steam off the mirror. She didn't want to know what
she looked like. She simply pulled on the clothes,
brushed her teeth and towel-dried her hair, then
combed it so it fell in ringlets.

Lex had obviously not heard her emerge. She saw
him through the open connecting door, sitting in the
chair by the window, bent over with his head in his
hands—a posture of utter despair or exhaustion.

She went toward him, padding quietly over the
rug in her bare feet, and was nearly upon him when
she somehow gave herself away. He raised his head.
Met her eyes.

There was no need for words. Kim went to him,
put her arms on his shoulders and sank down on his
knee so he could wrap her up, pull her close to him.
"That was bad," he said hoarsely, and pressed his
face into her shoulder.

Kim smoothed her hand over his back, laid her

cheek against the top of his head. His short cut bristled into her cheek. "It's over now."

"Not in my head. I just keep seeing it blow, over and over and over."

"How did you see it blow? I thought you were at the office."

"I was on my way to your apartment when the news came about Scott, so I got on the phone with you immediately. I wasn't more than five miles away."

"Why didn't you talk me through defusing that bomb?"

He raised his head abruptly. "Did you *see* your partner, Kim?"

"Yeah, but I defused the other one."

"I was with you. I knew what we were dealing with. All I knew about this one was that one just like it had blown the front of Scott's apartment across the street."

"Oh."

He took a breath, blew it out. His hand spread over her tummy. "I just…I know it's…I just couldn't have stood it…."

"I get it." Kim put her hand around his jaw. Whiskers poked her fingers. "Thank you," she whispered, and bent her head, and pressed her lips to his.

With a little explosion, her heart said, *oh, good.* He tasted of peppermint gum and salt, and he made a noise as she opened her mouth and let him in, his clever, hungry tongue, and his hand gripped her shoulder tight.

Kim said lightly, "Ow!"

He pulled back in a rush, and she grinned. "The shoulder is sore."

"Oh." His eyes slid down. "Where should I put my hands then? Show me a place that isn't sore."

"How about—" she guided his hand to her left breast "—here?"

"That works for me," he said, and pulled her down to his mouth again.

Me, too, Kim thought, arching into his palm, feeling the need for release building up, burning in her as he dragged a thumbnail over her nipple. She pressed closer, opened her mouth to the full thrust of his tongue, and pressed her thigh closer to the erection that was nudging her leg. He made a low noise, pushed his hand under her shirt, to bare skin.

A sharp knock sounded on the door. "Room service."

They parted, but slowly, dazedly. "I don't think we can do this, can we?" he asked.

"Let's eat and then see."

"I don't want—"

"Luthor, stop it. I'm not a delicate little flower."

He laughed. "Believe me, I know that." He pushed her off his lap. "Then let me get that, will ya? I'm starving."

* * *

They ate their supper and watched reruns of *Cheers* on television, and drank root beer out of the soda machines down the hall. It helped. Kim felt the shaky sense of disorientation leave her as food and her senses grounded her in the now.

Conversationally, she said, "You know, I have no idea where I'm going to live!" And then, "Oh, shit! I've got to call my mother right this minute." She hopped up, fully intending to go get her purse, and thus her cell phone, but both had, of course, been blown up. "I don't have a cell phone anymore."

"You can use mine."

"That's all right. I'll use the landline. I jus—" She took a breath. "I guess it's just sinking in, a little at a time. I don't have stuff anymore."

He gave her a sympathetic look, which was better than trying to offer condolences. He forked a dark green, dewy piece of steamed broccoli and admired it. "You had a big pile of knicky-knacky things under a table in your study. They're okay."

Kim nodded. "Cool. Thanks." She went to the other room and dialed her mother. "I'm fine, Mom," she said.

"What happened this time?"

"Oh, so you haven't seen the news today. Good. There was…um…a bomb in my apartment."

"Jesus, Mary and Joseph," her mother exclaimed. "You've got to find some other work, girl."

"We'll talk about that another day. I'm too tired tonight. I just wanted to give you the number where I am and let you know you shouldn't worry. Write this down," she said, and read her the number and room number of the hotel. "I'll be here for a little while, at least a few days. I'm probably not going back to the apartment."

"Come stay here."

"Mom. No way. Put you guys all in danger? I don't think so." She remembered that she'd promised to bring Scott there for dinner on Sunday, and the thought made her ache. "My partner was badly injured, Mom. Can you tell Nana to put him on her prayer lists? Scott Shepherd."

"Sure, baby. So how are you staying safe?"

"They have guards all over. The man who was in Chicago is here, too, right next door."

"Oh, that's good! Lex, right?"

How did she remember things like that? "Yeah. Don't get any ideas. I'm not marrying anybody, all right?"

"Okay, baby, don't get all excited. You can have your private life."

"Ha! What's that, a new ploy?"

Eileen laughed. "Keep me posted, honey, okay?"

"Will do, Ma. Love you." She hung up and realized there was one more call she had to make. This was somewhat delicate, but she had to call Marc. She should have called before this, in case he'd seen the news coming in from Chicago yesterday, but it would be unforgivable to leave it now. For a moment, she dithered over what to say to Lex, then finally decided on the truth.

She walked to the doorway between their rooms. "I had a sort of boyfriend and I have to call him. It's nothing serious, but it would be rude of me not to let him know I'm okay."

Lex half smiled. "Okay."

"I just thought I should tell you. In case the sound of the conversation is...well, intimate."

His smile broadened. "Okay. Thanks."

Kim waited a minute, then didn't know what she was waiting for, and turned around and went back to the phone. She called Marc's number and it picked up on the third ring. "Hi, this is Marc Spinuzzi. I'm away on assignment in Peru until October 20. You may leave a message with my agent at 555-0931 if you have urgent material, otherwise, leave a message and I'll get back to you as soon as I can."

He checked messages when he could, mainly to keep the voice mail from overflowing. When the tone sounded, Kim said, "Hi, Marc. You probably haven't seen the news, but sooner or later you'll hear that I've been mixed up in some high-profile events. I just wanted to let you know that I'm okay. I lost my cell phone and my apartment is...um...messed up, so I didn't want you to worry."

She couldn't think what else to say. He was a good guy, but he wasn't *her* guy. Anymore. "Take care," she said, and hung up.

When she padded back into the other room, Lex had put his plate aside and was stretched out on the bed, his head propped up on pillows. "Everything okay?"

She nodded.

"Why don't you go to bed, Valenti? You're dead on your feet."

For a long moment, she looked at him. "Can I lie down beside you? Just for…companionship?"

Without a word, he opened his arm, made a space. Kim fell into it, settled her head on his shoulder and let go of a breath. "Thank you."

Beneath her ear, his voice rumbled. "No problem."

The round of his shoulder was exactly perfect for her head. Kim rested her palm over his ribs. "Once again, I would really love to make love to you, but my body is too exhausted."

"There's time. Go to sleep."

"I just wanted you to know—"

"I know, Kim. Sleep, sweetheart. You've had a long day, and I've got your back."

Only then did she close her eyes. "Thank you," she whispered. As she drifted off, a television commercial about scrubbing bubbles came on, and the song entered her drifting state. There was something she should be remembering, something important, something to do with those bubbles.

Whatever it was. was lost as she fell into the ocean of sleep, where nothing hurt and no one was critically injured and no one had died.

But only a minute into her sleep, she jolted awake, pulling away violently from the warmth and comfort of lying with Lex. "What am I doing?" she said, more to herself than him.

The sudden movement made her feel dizzy, and she swayed. Lex took her arm. "Hey. You okay? What's going on?"

She waved her hand "I can't sleep with you. It's one of my rules."

"Rules?"

Blinking, she nodded. "To keep things from getting too complicated. No sleeping together."

"I see." He sounded amused, and she glared at him.

"What?"

"Sweetheart, you are so wiped out. you can't even see straight. I'm not gonna bother you, but I think considering all you've been through the past few days, would it be so bad to just let go and let someone hold you?"

Kim wasn't sure. He made it sound so reasonable and obvious. But was there a trick in it? She couldn't think of one. She continued to peer at him, half-blind with exhaustion.

He slid down, pulled her arm, and she fell, like a stage hypnotist's subject, into a slump against his body. His arms went around her, making her feel safe and comfortable, and she really just couldn't think of a reason not to sleep with him.

As in *sleep*-sleep, not sex-sleep.

His body was lean and he smelled just right, and she put her hand on his flat belly. "You're kind of skinny, you know."

"Yeah. I eat and eat and it never gets better."

"It's all right. It's not a bad thing. I was just noticing." She traced the edge of his rib. "Is being skinny for guys like being plump for girls?"

He covered her hand with his own, spread his fingers over hers. "Pretty much."

"That was so awful today," she said in a hoarse voice. "Being trapped, like a coffin, like dying. I kept telling myself that it would be worse to be at the bottom of a building after an earthquake, and I thought of my brother getting beheaded, which was really a whole lot worse, and it didn't help."

"Your brother was beheaded?"

"Yeah. In Iraq."

"I'm so sorry, Kim."

"Thanks." She nestled closer, taking comfort and relief in the feel of his rib cage, his warmth. "I'm not there now," she said.

"No." His lips pressed warm against her temple. "You're safe now."

* * *

In her dream, Kim was kicking something, fighting her way out of a big sack of darkness. She could not breathe. Her voice made no sound. She flailed awake, screaming. sitting straight up.

Into a disorienting darkness she didn't recognize.

"Hey, hey, hey," said a voice, and a hand was on her back. "You're safe, honey. You're safe."

Lex. Hotel.

"Sorry," she whispered, and got up to get a drink of water.

In the bathroom, she turned on the light and reached for the water glass, wincing as she caught sight of her face, bruised and battered and swollen and discolored. "Cute, Valenti." she said, and drank deeply.

"You all right?" Lex called.

She stared at herself in the mirror. "Yeah, sorry. I didn't mean to wake you." She padded out into the bedroom. "I'll go sleep in the other room."

"Kim."

"What?"

"Come here."

For a minute, she hesitated. "I still don't want to make love, Lex."

"Will you let your guard down just one tiny bit, darlin'? I am not the bad guy."

She took a breath, let it out. Walked silently to the side of the bed. "What?"

He tugged her hand and she tumbled into the bed. "Lex, I—"

His mouth covered hers, that full, beautiful mouth. Kim felt something in her let go, and her arms lifted, went around his shoulders. "That's it," he whispered, and pressed their bodies together. She loved the way he felt, long and lean and strong, his big hands sliding down her hips, up again.

She didn't object when he tugged upward on her T-shirt and skimmed it over her head, and pressed his naked chest to her breasts. "That feels good," she whispered.

"Oh, yeah." His hands moved on her, smooth and easy. Kim opened her hands and stroked the glossy skin of his back, opening to the thrust of his tongue in her mouth.

"I changed my mind," she said, and wrapped her legs around his hips, and rocked against his erection.

"It's not necessary," he said over her lips. "What you need is the touch. It grounds you back here on this planet, in this life."

"Really." There was enough light that she could make out the ghostly edge of his cheekbone. "Is this bomb squad lore?"

"It is." He moved against her subtly, clasped her breast in his hand. "You can eat, too." Bent his head to her nipple and nibbled lightly. "Anything physical."

"Seems like having sex would be the best, then."

She pushed her hands into the back of his sweats, smoothed her hands along his butt. "Nice," she whispered, and kissed his shoulder, his neck. Lingered along his earlobe. "We can have that longest, best, sweatiest sex another time. Maybe tonight, I'd settle for the regular, ordinary kind."

"Regular?" he said with a smile in his voice. "Not with me, Wind Talker?"

"Show me."

He slid her pants from her and her panties, and Kim spread her legs for his long fingers to glide inside and coax her to ripeness, when she said, "Now, please," and he came home, the heft and length of him spearing her to the earth, to the physical, to the now. She was grounded in sweat and tongues and tangled legs, centered in the crush of his chest and his beard scraping over her chin, and the slow, fierce thrust of him inside of her, aligned by a violent orgasm that split through her, scalp to toes, and radiated from their joined bodies to her elbows, her knees, made her clasp him hard to her body, biting into his shoulder. He came then, too, rocking hard against her, his voice guttural and deep against her ear, as rich as fertile earth.

Kim breathed against him for a long time, taking pleasure in the ease of his shoulders, the familiarity of his breathing on her ear. "Not regular," she said at last. "But lovely."

"Mmm," he said, and she could hear him floating away. His lips moved on her neck. "Mmm."

She chuckled. "Get off me before you fall asleep and squash me."

"Okay. In a minute." He moved against her, squeezed her bottom. "You have the sweetest little body. I loved finding out you were so curvy."

"Thank you."

"The pleasure was mine," he said, and sighed, moving away.

Kim shifted, started to stand up. He grabbed her arms. "No, you don't."

"I was just going to the bathroom."

"No, you'll go to bed in the other room, and I want you here."

Kim felt a pang. "I don't sleep over," she said. But she didn't pull away when he steadily pulled on her body, tugging her down to him, close to his body, tucked in his arms.

"You are tonight."

She thought about moving, but it suddenly seemed too much trouble to disentangle herself from the net of his arms and legs. His body, damp and long, cradled her perfectly and he tucked her close like a stuffed animal. "I guess it won't hurt just this once."

Lex was already asleep.

She smiled. How like a man. Funny how little she minded this time.

Chapter 19

Saturday, October 9

In spite of the fact that it was Saturday, Kim and Lex arrived at the agency by eight. There were few regular personnel around, but a core group of FBI, CIA and NSA operatives had gathered in the conference room. Their job was to focus on and discuss the current situation with the Berzhaan terrorist cell.

As they walked down the hall, Lex paused at Scott's desk. "I'm going to see what he was tracking down yesterday. He seemed pretty sure of some site possibilities."

"Sure." Carrying a latte from Starbucks, Kim

popped her head into the conference room. "Do I have time to make a phone call to the hospital? I want to find out how my partner is doing."

Agent Rosen from the Washington branch of the FBI, a tall, craggy-faced man in his fifties, nodded gravely. "We're just getting everyone up to speed. Take your time."

"Thanks. I won't be long." She dropped her things on the desk, glanced at a small pile of pink reminder notes, most dealing with various e-mail files she needed to examine for the case and picked up the phone to dial the hospital.

Scott's condition was critical but stable, the same as the night before. She gritted her teeth, thinking of his missing hand, and wanted to kill someone.

Which wasn't the answer, either. Mansour was seeking revenge for his lost family, killing because those he loved had been killed. If she wanted to kill in revenge, too, when would it ever end? Someone had once said, if you keep following an eye for an eye, pretty soon everyone is blind.

She wanted to stop the violence. Stop the maiming and injury of innocents. Not create more.

Quickly, she opened the e-mail files that had been flagged and skimmed them. There was a lot of work to be done today. First, she'd go to the meeting, see what the team had come up with, then she would come back and sort through this material.

Picking up the file she and Scott had assembled

yesterday, she went to the conference room and entered quietly, sliding into an open chair that was as far as she could get from Lex. The one thing she didn't want was a rumor mill churning out gossip about the two of them.

She counted seven agents altogether, two women, five men. Kim had worked with three of them before. She didn't recognize the others. Agent Rosen had tacked a giant map of the United States on the wall and was busy sticking bubble-head pins in various locations.

When he turned around, he spied Kim and said, "Good, we're all here now. I'll introduce you all. This is Kim Valenti, who originally broke the code and tracked the terrorist cell to Chicago."

A ripple of interest and respect went around the table. Kim lifted a hand. "My partner, Scott Shepherd, also broke the code—though I do wish I hadn't said so publicly."

"We're all very sorry to hear of his injuries. How is he this morning?"

She shrugged. "About the same. Not good. Let's get these guys, huh?"

Rosen introduced the rest of the group, assembled for their expertise in various areas. Lex was the explosives expert, Kim the cryptographer and linguist. Others on the team included a structural engineer, a security officer and an expert on the culture and religion of the country of Berzhaan.

Rosen was reviewing the information collected thus far—the same material Scott, Lex and Kim had been reviewing the day before. He was reviewing the possible targets, and sticking pins in them. "There are any number of large parades taking place on Monday, which is Columbus Day, and we don't really know exactly what this cell might do, or if there are multiple targets. Thanks to Agent Ramirez—" a small dark man nodded "—we've pinpointed the most dramatic parades in various cities. We're particularly interested in those where the clash between Italian and Native American communities is pretty fierce, year after year, because security will be focused on keeping the peace with that, and a suicide bomber can do a lot of damage in a big crowd." He pushed pins into the map, narrating aloud the spots: "Denver, Seattle, Minneapolis."

Kim scribbled notes.

Rosen continued, sticking pins into cities where there were important military or transportation bridges: Coronado Bay in San Diego, Houston Ship Channel Bridge, Bay and Golden Gate Bridges, George Washington. "Any others you can think of?"

"How about the Lenny Zakim Bridge in Boston?" said the structural engineer. "It's pretty dramatic, and well-known."

"Right." He stuck a pin in.

There was more discussion about the various possibilities, until the map was bristling like a porcupine. "Obviously, we're going to have to narrow this down some. Let's go back through the materials we have and see what stands out."

Kim glanced at Lex to see if he would share anything from the thick file in front of him. He shook his head minutely and shifted his eyes toward the door. She understood the message: they would discuss it alone.

"I have a giant pile of e-mails that came in over the past twenty-four hours," Kim said. "I'm wondering if it might be better to see if we can track down the headquarters of this group before they make their move."

Rosen nodded, as did several others. "We know they were in Chicago. Any indications of other locales?"

Dee Hazzard, the cultural anthropologist said, "We've been tracking a man out of Portland, John Hallam. He spent much of his youth in the Middle East with his father and has known ties to a rebel sect connected to the Keminis. He was arrested twice in connection with various criminal activities both in the U.S. and abroad. He resurfaced unexpectedly three days ago, in the hostage situation at UBS." She pulled out his picture and held it up.

Kim recognized the manager of the station the night Mansour took over. "He escaped that night, with Mansour and Dunst, didn't he?"

"Yes. But we think he's taken an Islamic name, Afzal Abd-Al-Aziz."

Kim wrote the name down. "Hmm. He thinks well of himself—the name means superior and servant of the powerful. "

"One of our agents thinks he might be living with a woman in Brooklyn."

"Can't we just go in there, then?"

"Not just yet. The woman is the daughter of a highly placed Saudi businessman who is easily offended, and the feds don't want to cross him unless we have to."

"Even if a bridge gets blown up?"

The woman shrugged a little.

Lex spoke up. "Shepherd had gone through a lot of material over the past week. He felt the terrorists were going to hit in several spots, but the main one will be the George Washington Bridge, on Columbus Day."

Hazzard nodded. "It has the biggest American flag in the country. We need to get extra security up there."

Something was bothering Kim about the entire discussion. What was off-kilter? "It's almost like they've drawn us a map, don't you think?"

Rosen pursed his lips. "That's not uncommon."

"True, but I think we're dealing with someone here who is a lot smarter than the average bear. He's determined to make a statement, and he's not going to take a chance that we'll figure it out before he gets there."

"So, you think it *won't* be a bridge?"

"I don't know. I just think we need to be wary about jumping to conclusions." She thought of Scott, thought of the hostages at the television station, of the men with their assault weapons. "These guys really want to do some damage—where can they do the most? Where will it be the most dramatic?"

"Excellent questions." Rosen looked at his watch. "Let's get busy and meet back here late this afternoon. No detail should go unnoticed. And in the meantime, I'll get a man to alert the police in every city in the country that has a Columbus Day parade, both tomorrow and Monday. They need to be aware of moving vans, correct? Anything else that's come up in the intelligence?"

"Denver is always a hot spot," Kim said. "My partner is from there, and a reference to the American Indian Moment alerted him to the possibility of parades being targeted. AIM uses Denver as a showcase for their political objections to Columbus."

"All right, let's get to work, see what we can find out, turn up on all of this," Rosen said "I want a list of all the parades in the country, and anything unusual about any of them."

"So, it's bridges and Columbus Day now?" one agent asked. "How can we cover all those possibilities in one day?"

"We can't," Rosen said. "Let's just do our best. Maybe we'll get lucky."

Chapter 20

Back at her desk, Kim settled for a minute and stared at the computer screen. What were they missing? What link would lead them to the true targets in time to stop any violence?

"Look through the top to the middl'a things...."

Lex dropped into the chair beside the desk. "Hey. I don't think it's the bridge, either. Let's toss it back and forth for a minute, d'you mind?"

"No." She threw a pencil down on top of the papers. "Hallam—the American from the television station—is obviously a mastermind, and he's mixed up with a very wealthy Saudi woman. Maybe that's where the cash is coming from."

"No doubt that's at least some of it. It's also seems that this—" he consulted his notes "—Richard Dunst is selling arms in Berzhaan. Arms deals are always worth a bundle."

"That's all fine, but it's not solving the immediate problem, which is—where are these guys?"

"I don't buy the Brooklyn connection," Lex said. "It's all just too pat."

"I know. Like somebody is standing there, waving their arms saying, 'Look over here! This is where we're going to strike!' They aren't that obvious." She flipped through some of the e-mails on her desk, skimming the highlighted information. "We have so little on Mansour, and he's the real mastermind here."

"What do you have?"

Kim punched a button on the computer and called up a file. She knew most of it, but didn't want to miss anything. She reiterated the information Oracle had sent. "This is where we need to focus," she said. "Mansour is going to take something down this weekend, and he'll be smart about it."

"I'd love to get my hands on the bastard."

Kim thought of Scott, thought of being beneath the desk, nearly smothering, thought of the hostages in the television station. "He's very dangerous," she agreed. "We need to get him." She tucked her hair behind one ear. "You can use Scott's computer—let's see what we can gather about Mansour himself, and see if we can get inside his mind."

"Is there a profiler on this case?"

"That's Hazzard," Kim said.

"All right." He rolled up the papers in his hand and popped her lightly on the hand. "Talk at you later."

The first thing Kim did was to head for AA.gov, the Athena Academy Web site, and hope she could get some information that way. Because her home terminals had been destroyed, she didn't know how to get in the back door without leaving the agency. The footprint technologies were so high for security reasons that Kim could not—as she had from Lex's apartment—access the Oracle site. Instead, she posted an innocuous note on the Athena bulletin board.

TO: All
FROM: Kim Valenti, Class of 199—
SUBJECT: Need info on Fathi bin Amin Mansour
Urgent—need anything anyone can deliver on above named Berzhaan native. Educated in England, now in U.S. Present at UBC television hostage situation, suspected of other plots. Currently on the loose.

She added her phone number and e-mail address, and hoped it would be enough to attract the attention of Delphi, who could then perhaps call or give further instructions.

In the meantime, she sorted through the information and read the file for Mansour one more time. The information from Oracle was included:

> Mansour is prodigiously intelligent. Advanced degrees from Oxford in chemical engineering and European history. Mother and two brothers killed in guerilla raids by the Keminis four years ago, for which he holds the West responsible. He is connected to several bombings. His whereabouts are unknown. (See attached photograph taken in London, 2001.)

Kim flipped through the rest—a transcribed text from the television station takeover, a dossier from Interpol, showing connections to Chicago.

Nothing they didn't already know.

Lex suddenly appeared. "Want to know where the candidates are speaking this weekend?"

Kim raised her eyebrows. "Sure."

"Baltimore and Washington, D.C."

"Damn." She chewed the inside of her cheek. "I really oughta take myself off this case right now. My partner was nearly killed. My apartment has been blown up, and now my little sisters are on that parade route."

"You can't get off the case now, Valenti. We need you."

"I know." She rubbed her face, flipped another page over on the dossier in front of her and stared at the transcript of her conversation with Karl Gibson, the police officer in New York City. A lost piece of information slid into place suddenly. "Hang on," she said to Lex. "I think I just figured something out." Urgently, she dialed the number for Gibson. When he answered, she said, "Hello, Mr. Gibson. Kim Valenti from the NSA. Quick question—what was the name of the tire shop you raided near the George Washington bridge?"

"Hold on. I can get that for you in two seconds." Kim waited.

"Here it is—Hafiz's Tires."

"Thank you very much, Mr. Gibson. You might have saved the day."

"Hope so. It'd be the easiest save ever."

She chuckled, put the phone down and picked it up again. "This is probably too easy," Kim said, "but you never know." She flipped her Rolodex and punched in some numbers.

A hated voice at the other end of the line said, "This is Dana Milosovich. Please leave your number at the sound of the tone. If this is an emergency, dial 326."

"Damn." She couldn't technically call it an emergency.

"What's up?" Lex said.

"I'm looking for the name of a tire shop owned by one of the terrorists in Chicago." She picked up the piece of paper. "Any chance you know of a Hafiz Tires?"

Lex raised his brows. "I actually do. It's not far from the UBC station Why?"

"We need to see if there's a Hafiz Tires in any of our targeted locations, especially in Baltimore and D.C." She nodded toward a chair by her desk. "Sit down. The fastest way to do this is the Internet."

Into Google, Kim typed "Hafiz Tires," and entered it.

A list of six matches came up. "There it is," she said grimly. "Hafiz Tires on—" she rolled her eyes "—President Street."

Lex was already on his feet.

"The parade goes right by there," Kim said, standing. "Let's take a look."

Lex stuck his head in the conference room. "We've got a lead to check out. Have backup ready for our call."

Kim drove since she knew the area. Traffic on the freeways was not heavy, and they made good time into town, but as they moved into downtown Baltimore their luck thinned. The Inner Harbor area, always popular with tourists, was doubly clogged. "This didn't used to be such a huge thing," she said, tapping her fingers against the steering wheel. "Past couple of years, everybody in the neighborhood has gone all out—breakfasts, spaghetti dinners, Sons of Italy and all the beauty queens."

"It's pretty crowded."

Someone honked behind her, and Kim made a

gesture with her hands. "I can only move as fast as the traffic, buddy."

Lex chuckled. "Getting a little aggressive out here in the old neighborhood, sister."

"Ha, ha." Spying an alley, she made a sudden decision. "I bet I can get us out of this car in three minutes." She turned into the narrow alley, which looked like a dead end. When she eased by a cluster of Dumpsters, however, there was a second alley off to the right. "Aha!" she cried in satisfaction. "One of my brothers used to have a girlfriend who lived in that building," she said, and pointed to a series of windows. The alley opened into a lot behind a small grocer's, packed with cars. From the other side, it would have appeared to be full, but Kim eased into a spot next to an SUV. "Victory," she said. "And we're not even stuck here."

"Good work."

"We're going to have to hike a little ways," she said, climbing out of the car. A chill wind bit through her coat. She shivered a little, then zipped it up.

"You're the boss." He zipped up his coat, too, and pulled a cap out of his pocket, tugging it down over his ears. As they came out onto the street, with a view of the harbor barely visible through breaks in the buildings, he said, "Nice."

"It can be."

Kim turned, turned again, led them down side streets that were less crowded. The area was noisy

with voices and children, anticipation. They passed
a restaurant advertising a pancake breakfast, and the
line was still into the street. Kim inhaled. "That
smells great."

They took a left onto President Street. About a block
down, Kim suddenly stopped, looking at the building
on the corner. "This is it." It was painted a sunny yellow, and had been neatly painted with the name of the
shop in English with Arabic flourishes and a little icon
of a small man smiling and rolling a tire along. "Hafiz's
Tires. This wasn't here the last time I was in the neighborhood." The showroom area was dark, and a sign in
the window said Closed For The Holiday Weekend.
She looked up at the multipaned windows. A light was
on inside. "Someone may be in there."

"Come on," Lex said, and they walked quickly
around the corner, toward the back of the shop.

Kim moved along behind Lex as he went into the
alley. A window faced the alley and Lex started to
make a leap for the windowsill, then swore and held
up his injured hand. "You're going to have to look."
He knelt, making a step out of his leg, and Kim
climbed on it, reached for the ledge, and slowly
pulled herself up to peek in the window.

What she could see was a garage area, wide-open,
with three men clustered around something in the
middle of the room. She recognized two of them—
one was Mansour; the other was Ugly Face from the
television station. Another knot, mostly younger

men, Berzhaanians by the look of them, stood to one side, smoking. A moving van, painted yellow, was parked in one of the bays. Her stomach flipped.

Kim lowered herself. "It's our guys, all right." She brushed off her palms. "And I think they've got a bomb in there."

"How many of them?"

"Three, plus four foot soldiers." She described the scenario inside.

He met her eyes. "Call for backup." He reached behind himself and pulled out a pistol.

Kim got out her cell phone and quietly relayed what they'd found and the need for stealth.

"They're on the way." Her breath came out of her mouth in puffs of fog.

Lex moved from foot to foot, his injured right hand tucked under his coat. The tip of his nose had grown red with the cold. "If there are any armed bombs in there, this could get ugly," he said.

"Just don't send me to a corner to cover my head with pillows," she said, her eyes on the front of the building.

"Are you going to forgive me for that?"

"Probably," she said. "Eventually."

"That sounds promising."

Kim looked at him. "You know, I saw what the bomb did to Scott, but he didn't know it was there. He pulled the door and got blown up. I would have appreciated the chance to try and disarm the one in my condo."

"I know. But let me tell you, darlin', I wouldn't have been able to disarm it. The first rule in dealing with bombs is to know your limits."

Kim nodded. Maybe she was being a little touchy. "This is really too close to home for my tastes. My sisters are going to be in that parade on Monday, and these guys might have killed them. That makes me very angry."

"I can understand that."

She looked around, from the treetops glowing against the sky, to the hint of water in the air from the harbor. "Why here, anyway? Why this parade, why not something more important?"

"Your problem, Valenti, is that you're expecting terrorists to be reasonable and think like the general population. Fanaticism is the opposite of reasonable." His jaw tightened. "I remember when there were always a bunch of Irish kids getting killed. And the Rwandans in the lake...how many people were slaughtered in that debacle? A lot."

Kim nodded.

"So you just say to yourself, these guys aren't reasonable, and you do your best to keep them from doing any damage."

"Right." She took a breath. "Well, Superman, you ready to get the bad guy?"

"Don't do anything stupid, all right? I don't want to have to kick your ass when we're finished here."

She gave him a sideways smile. "No promises. If anybody bumps my ear, they're dead."

For a long moment, he looked down at her. "Ah, hell, Valenti, why'd you have to go and get under my skin, huh?" He looped his arm around her neck and kissed her, hard.

Suddenly, the idea of him getting hurt in there was not acceptable. "I'll check on backup."

He let her go. "Do it."

Kim dialed the office and put the phone to her ear, stepping away to look around the building.

Suddenly, the side door opened. Kim simultaneously slammed the folding phone to its off position and dived behind the corner of the building, gesturing fiercely to Lex. She put her finger to her mouth.

Three of the younger men spilled out, their backs to Kim And Lex, talking quietly among themselves, as if it were just an ordinary day and they were going out to get some food for the transmission crew. She could only catch a word or two, their voices thinning as they walked away.

Maybe, she thought, there was no bomb. Maybe it was a headquarters of some sort, a rendezvous place.

Lex pushed around her and grabbed the door before it closed entirely.

She nodded. She eased in first, slipping behind the truck. The three men in the center of the warehouse were helping a young man, a boy, really, into a vest with bulging pockets.

She looked over her shoulder just as one of the young men who'd left stepped back in and charged at Lex.

Jumping out of sight, Kim looked around the immediate environment for a weapon. A heavy steel bar was propped against the wall and she grabbed it. She peeked around the truck in time to see the youth on the ground, unconscious or dead, and Lex dashing into the open, yelling at the top of his voice, gun trained on the startled terrorists. Lex knocked one down and away from the boy before he could move, his gun pointed at the sober-eyed Mansour, who raised his hands.

None of them saw Kim, coming from the other side as Ugly Face drew a gun. She was not at all unhappy to have to slam him with the bar across the shoulders. He fell hard and the gun skittered across the concrete floor. She knelt and grabbed it, just as Ugly started to clamber to his feet. With a sharp kick to the chest, she knocked him down.

He dived away from her, and remembering the struggle in the television station, Kim took no chances. She slammed the butt of the gun down on his head, and he collapsed, unconscious.

"Hands on your head!" she cried to the boy in the loaded flak jacket. Slowly, he obeyed, his eyes sullen and liquid. In Arabic, she added, "And, boy, don't you move one muscle, do you hear me?"

His nostrils flared, but he stood there without moving.

And then backup arrived in force.

Ugly Face looked as if he had a concussion. Mansour would not meet her eyes.

She'd get to that in a minute.

First, with her eyes on the truck in front of her, she strode over to Lex. "Cell phone, please."

He pulled it out, his own eyes on the mountains of explosives wired to the truck. He sighed as Kim punched in numbers. "Good God."

Kim dialed the office and asked to be put through to the team leader. "Agent Rosen," she said. "Better get some teams nationwide to check out all tire chops called Hafiz's Tires. Pronto." As she spoke, the third man in the trio was boring holes through her with dark, angry eyes. "Hafiz, I presume?" she said to him.

He spit on the ground at her feet. Kim smiled faintly. "You have no idea how glad I am to bring you down. And how pleased I am that you could not martyr yourself killing innocents."

"There are no innocent Americans." The comment came from Mansour, standing next to Hafiz with calm dignity, his large eyes liquid and fierce in a well-cut face. "All bear the guilt of murder in Berzhaan."

"You know," she said, tucking her hair away from

her face, "I am sorry for your loss, Mr. Mansour. I can see it caused you terrible pain, and I'm sorry you had to endure it. I've lost someone, too, and sometimes his face keeps me up at night." She frowned. "But can you tell me how you killing my sisters will bring yours back? How is it ever going to make anything better?"

Maybe she'd hoped for a flicker of repentance, or guilt, or sorrow. "Ask your country," he said. "Ask them when they will stop funding rebels to kill our wives and daughters and sisters. When they stop, we will stop."

Kim shook her head. She glanced at the third man, the stiff-faced man she'd struggled with at the television station. "And you—may you burn forever, wherever it is."

He didn't bother with a reply, and the police led the trio and the young boy away.

Lex said beside her, "Nice try. Now, let's get to work."

"What kind of bombs do we have today? Bomb caps? Time pencils? Plastic? What?"

He grinned. "C'mon, little girl, let me show you." His eyebrow wiggled

Chapter 22

Election Day

After a dinner of homemade raviolis and at least a quart of red wine, and rolls as fluffy as cotton candy, and bowls of buttered carrots and green beans, Kim sat on the couch in her mother's living room and tried to keep from groaning.

On her right, Lex had no such qualms. He sprawled, all six foot four of him, limbs akimbo, across the couch, rubbing his belly every so often. "Mama Eileen, that was so good." He reached out and snared her hand as she was about to pass, and kissed her knuckles. "Thank you."

Kim gave him a look. "No," she said to forestall the next question. "I will not marry you."

"What if I cooked like your mama?"

"Not even then."

On her left, Scott chuckled. He was very thin, and had not fully recovered his strength after being in the hospital for nearly three weeks, but he was on the mend. The doctors expected it would be at least a year before he was back to his former health, but Scott had vowed to make it six months. She believed he could do it.

A graphic came on the television they were all watching. "It appears we will not have to hold back our prediction of who will be the next president of the United States," the anchor said. "After tallying votes in just six states, incumbent president can*not* hope to surpass the electoral votes now amassed by opponent, Gabriel Monihan. The race goes to the new president of the United States of America, President Gabriel Monihan."

Kim jumped up and did a little dance around the room. "Whoohoo! The bastard is gone!"

"Kim!" her mother said.

She laughed and kissed her sisters on the cheek. "Cut it out!" cried Jenni.

"You've never heard that before, huh?"

Behind her, Lex whistled and clapped, and she gave him a kiss on the cheek, too. Then Scott, who looked disgruntled said, "We can't have a president who is that young. It's just not right."

Kim grinned and kissed him, too. "You'll just have to be the most handsome president ever, not the youngest."

He winked.

"In other news," the announcer said, "terrorists suspected of nefarious activities within the U.S. have been arraigned in Washington, D.C."

Kim turned to see the photo of the elegant Mansour flash over the screen. Video of him in orange prison clothes, his hair too long, made her sad. "He had so much potential," she said. "And how did he use it? Killing people, destroying the world instead of trying to make it better."

Eileen jumped up, wary as always when the subject turned to terrorism and soldiers. "Anyone want coffee?"

"Let me help you," Scott said, and hauled himself to his feet.

Behind Kim, Lex said quietly, "Come sit down, honey."

The pain was finally starting to emerge, like a splinter working its way to the surface—for the past few weeks, Kim had been overflowing with grief for her brother, Jason. It was healthier than the bottled-up agony she'd felt before that, but it still wasn't comfortable, and something about Mansour always made her think of her lost, beloved brother.

She sat down and rested in the circle of comfort Lex provided. "It gets easier," he said. "I promise."

"I know," Kim returned and put her hand on his long and sexy thigh. "Thanks."

"No problem," he said, and settled his hand in a comforting way over her once-torn ear. It was protective and sweet and she appreciated it.

"You're all right, Lex Luthor," Kim said.

"You, too, Wind Talker."

You won't want to miss
the next thrilling
ATHENA FORCE
adventure!
Turn the page for
a special excerpt from

TARGET by Cindy Dees

On sale May 2005
At your favorite retail outlet.

Chapter 1

3:00 a.m.

Diana Lockworth lurched bolt upright in bed. She blinked, disoriented, at the blanket of darkness around her. Something had ripped her from a deep, dreaming slumber to full consciousness. But what? Even the street outside was quiet, deserted at this hour. Silence pressed against her eardrums. *Nothing*.

She flopped back down on her pillow in disgust. The telltale whirl of disjointed thoughts in her head did not bode well for getting back to sleep anytime soon. Crud. She propped herself up on an elbow to plump her squashed eiderdown pillow. And heard a noise. Either the biggest mouse in the history of mankind was in her house, or else someone had just bumped into something in her living room.

Intruder. Autonomic responses programmed into her relentlessly since she was a child kicked in. She rolled fast, flinging herself off the far side of the bed. Someone was out there. She could feel it.

She reached up onto her nightstand for the telephone, her hands shaky, and dialed 9-1-1. She whispered into the receiver, "There's someone in my house."

The 9-1-1 dispatcher efficiently asked her address, name, physical description and current location in her home. He was in the middle of telling her the police would be there in under five minutes when Diana heard another noise. The distinctive metallic squeak of her computer chair in the other room as someone sat down in it. She heard a faint, rapid clicking. Typing! *On her computer full of sensitive and highly dangerous material.*

She pushed upright, the phone forgotten, her bare feet silent on the hardwood floor. On bent knees, she raced catlike to the bedroom door. She opened it inch by cautious inch. A fast spin out into the hall. *Empty.* She plastered herself against the wall and tiptoed toward a blue glow emanating from the computer workstation in her living room. She leaped forward, surging into the living room on a wave of fury and fear.

One male, dressed in black. A black ski mask

over his face. He jumped to his feet and spun to face her in a fighting crouch.

She settled herself before the intruder. He rocked on the balls of his feet, noncommittal about attacking. She didn't want this guy to flee. She wanted to know who he was. Why he was poking around on her computer. She needed him to stand and fight.

"You think you can take me?" she taunted. "Think again. You're not man enough."

The guy snarled audibly. Excellent.

She laughed derisively. And that did it. The guy came in with a kick aimed at her face. She ducked under it easily and stiff-armed him in the sternum. He staggered backward. But to his credit, he came out swinging. Fast hands.

He was too close. She couldn't avoid the tackle. They both went down on the floor. She got an elbow between them, but the guy was pissed off now. He went for her neck with his gloved hands. She heaved and came around hard with her elbow. And clocked him in the jaw. The guy reeled back. A mighty shove and he was off her. She jumped to her feet.

"Who do you work for?" she demanded.

The guy's lip curled and he did a nifty back-bend-and-jump-to-his-feet move. Damn. She should've stood on his head while she had him down. He launched at her with a flurry of kicks and punches that forced her to give ground. She banged into the coffee table. Knocked it over. Stumbled over it and righted herself barely in time to get a hand up as he charged her. At the last second, he veered left and took off for the door. She pushed up and gave chase, bursting out onto her front porch. There! To the left. A sprinting figure.

She charged after him, the concrete sidewalk rough and cold beneath her bare feet. He screeched to a stop by the door of a car. Ripped it open and jumped in. The car peeled away from the curb.

She watched the vehicle turn onto River Road. Gone. The bastard had gotten away.

And she was standing in the middle of the street on a freezing January night in nothing but a cropped T-shirt and soft cotton short-shorts.

She hurried back inside and threw on a pair of jeans, and a T-shirt. She pulled her wavy, shoulder-length blond hair back into a ponytail and checked the spot on the back of her head where she'd hit the floor. No goose egg forming.

A chiming noise sounded. The doorbell. She moved carefully through the living room so as not to destroy evidence and opened the front door.

"You reported an intruder in your house, ma'am?" one officer asked tersely.

She nodded and stepped aside to let the pair of policemen inside. Quickly, she relayed what had happened.

"And you fought him off?" the first guy asked, sounding surprised.

"That's right."

"I'm Officer Grady and this is my partner, Officer Fratiano. Tell us exactly what happened again, and this time include every detail you can remember."

The poor cops scribbled busily until she was done with her trained observations, and no doubt they had a good case of writer's cramp. Grady moved around the room, notepad in hand, walking through the events she'd described. And then he looked up at her, skeptical. "I've never seen a victim of an attack who could describe it in such perfect detail. Your account jives exactly with the evidence. Almost too exactly." He paused and then added slyly, "That usually indicates the crime scene was a setup."

The guy thought she was lying about the intruder? She frowned and looked around the living room. It did look shockingly undisturbed. The upended coffee table and a few sofa pillows on the floor were the extent of the damage. She explained carefully, "I'm an Army Intelligence officer. I'm trained to notice details, even under duress."

"Mind if we have a look around, ma'am?" Grady asked dryly.

"Not at all," she answered coolly. *Jerk.*

Grady wandered down the hall toward her bedroom while the second officer checked her computer for fingerprints with a special flashlight.

"Hey, Vinny!" Officer Grady shouted from her bedroom. "Come have a look at this!"

Cripes. She winced. They'd found her wall of pictures. She hastened after Officer Fratiano to explain herself before they hauled her in as a stalker. She rounded the corner into her bedroom and, sure enough, the two cops were gaping at her massive collection of pictures of Gabe Monihan, President-elect of the United States. She had literally hundreds of pictures of him pinned up on the wall of her bedroom opposite her bed. They'd been taken mostly in the final months of last year's presidential campaign—the months leading up to and immediately after a bomb scare at Chicago's O'Hare airport that he'd gotten caught in the middle of. The incident had occurred just a couple weeks before the presidential election, and many pundits credited sympathy votes for Monihan. She had other theories on the incident, however.

"Are you some kind of sicko, lady?" Grady demanded.

She schooled her voice to patience. "I'm a conspiracy theorist for the government. I'm investigating the attack on Monihan last October. These pictures are part of my research."

"Research. Right," Grady growled. "Then you won't mind if we photograph all…this?"

"Go right ahead," she replied evenly.

God, she hated not being taken seriously. It was endemic to her work that people routinely thought she was crazy. But that was her job. To cook up crazy ideas and build contingency plans to respond to them.

In a decidedly rebellious frame of mind, she stood by silently while Grady and Fratiano painstakingly photographed her wall of pictures. They took their sweet time finishing the job. Finally, Grady said casually, "Any chance we could take those pictures with us?"

"No!" she answered sharply. "I told you. They're part of an ongoing investigation I'm conducting. Get a warrant if you want to seize any of my stuff."

Any pretense of pleasantry between them gone, the police left quickly after that. Some help they'd turned out to be.

She gave the Army Criminal Investigation Division a ring. A night sergeant took down the information about her break-in and, after she assured him no classified information had been stored on her home computer, seemed totally unimpressed by her urgency over someone attempting to break into said computer. When the guy asked which of her files had been accessed, she jolted. That was a darned good question. She promised to check out her system and get back to him on it.

She hung up the phone and sat down at her computer, checking out her basic operating system first. Yup, the code had been tampered with. The guy had been trying to gain access to her encrypted notes on dozens of possible conspiracies. *And that would be why they're encrypted, buddy.* The hacker's new commands inserted into her system were spare. Elegant. Coldly logical. This guy had a distinctive flair for his work. A strong signature to his programming style. Unfortunately, she didn't know the individual to whom it belonged.

She highlighted the intruder's code, then cut and pasted it to a new file. She'd have to show it around. See if any of her cyber pals recognized the work. In the meantime, it was wicked late and tomorrow was a big day. January 20. Inauguration day for her favorite poster boy.

She climbed into bed wearily and reached for the lamp beside her bed. "G'night, gorgeous," she mumbled at the wall of pictures of Monihan.

She closed her eyes gratefully and let her mind drift toward sleep.

She was just on the verge of slipping into unconsciousness when a sound jolted her rudely to full awareness. An insistent electronic chirping. *Now* what?

She padded out into the living room and stopped cold at her fully lit computer screen and the bold announcement across it in large letters that she had an incoming e-mail. When in the Sam Hill had her Internet server started announcing incoming messages like this? She went to the mail screen and gaped at the address of the e-mail's sender. Delphi@oracle.org.

Holy…freaking…cow.

Oracle? To her home address?

And *Delphi?* Personally?

An involuntary shiver passed through her. Oracle. An idea. A database. A secret organization. Her secondary employer and the tool of a shadowy figure known to her only as Delphi.

She'd been recruited for her ultrasecret work for Oracle and Delphi straight out of her army intelligence training. Although, she always suspected it was more her attendance at the exclusive Athena Academy for the Advancement of Women than her position in the government that earned her the nod from Oracle.

Delphi took intelligence from a wide variety of government and nongovernment sources and analyzed the staggering mass of information, combing through it all for hints of possible threats to the United States. The ultimate conspiracy theorist, as it were.

And tonight, Delphi had something to tell her. Hastily, she opened the e-mail.

Have been working on the database and it came up with a rather alarming bit of information. Could you please look into it immediately?—D

Attached was a reference number for the particular analysis Delphi wanted her to check out.

What in the world could be so urgent? Thoroughly alarmed now, Diana accessed Oracle's database and plugged in the reference number.

The threat analysis popped up onto the screen. She scrolled down through the lengthy write-up to the end where the thumbnail summary of the problem was traditionally placed. Tonight, this section was surprisingly short. She scanned the words quickly. And lurched upright in her seat at the report's terse conclusion.

A person or persons will attempt to assassinate President-elect Gabriel Monihan within the next twenty-four hours. You must stop them.

* * * * *

SILHOUETTE BOMBSHELL BRINGS YOU A FRESH VOICE IN ROMANTIC SUSPENSE....

She didn't know who to trust.

When her father had died tragically at the hands of an assassin, Sabrina Sullivan had given up her dream of working for the CIA and entered a quiet life with a new identity. Now her sister had been kidnapped and she'd been forced to return to her former life. But could she trust the man who'd replaced her father, or was she working with the enemy?

PARALLEL LIES
by Kate Donovan
(May 2005, SB #44)

Available at your favorite local retailer.

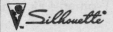

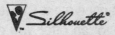
SPECIAL EDITION™

presents the next three books
in the continuity

MONTANA MAVERICKS

GOLD RUSH GROOMS
Lucky in love—and striking it rich—
beneath the big skies of Montana!

THEIR UNEXPECTED FAMILY
by **Judy Duarte**
SE #1676, on sale April 2005

CABIN FEVER
by **Karen Rose Smith**
SE #1682, on sale May 2005

And the exciting conclusion

MILLION-DOLLAR MAKEOVER
by **Cheryl St.John**
SE #1688, on sale June 2005

**Don't miss these thrilling stories—
only from Silhouette Books.**

Available at your favorite retail outlet.

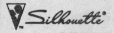

COMING NEXT MONTH

#41 SOPHIE'S LAST STAND by Nancy Bartholomew

Threats, stalkings, exploding cars—Sophie Mazaratti had had enough! And the formerly mild schoolteacher was taking matters into her own hands. Her sleazy ex-husband had sicced both the mob and the FBI on her, and the detective handling her case was making her rethink her vow of celibacy—but no one would stop Sophie from getting her life back on *her* terms....

#42 TARGET by Cindy Dees

Athena Force

Army intelligence captain Diana Lockworth had uncovered a plan to assassinate the president-elect of the United States—but no one believed her. She had only twenty-four hours to figure out who was behind the plot, where they planned to strike—and how to stop them. With the hours ticking away, Diana had to get the president himself on her side, and rely on her own ingenuity to save the day....

#43 THE AMAZON STRAIN by Katherine Garbera

Dr. Jane Miller had made her career by creating vaccines for lethal viruses, but she hadn't counted on having to travel to the Amazon Basin to administer the latest cure herself. Racing through the jungle to prevent a deadly outbreak, she soon learned that other people had their own agendas—and they'd do anything to stop Jane from reaching her goal....

#44 PARALLEL LIES by Kate Donovan

Her father had trained her to be the perfect spy. But when he died tragically at the hands of an assassin, Sabrina Sullivan had given up her dream of working for the CIA and entered a quiet life with a new identity. Now her sister had been kidnapped— and Sabrina suspected her father's killer was involved. Coming out of hiding to take on the secrets and lies from her former life, could she trust the man who'd replaced her father, or was she working with the enemy?